CABIN 3

STEELE SHADOWS SECURITY

AMANDA MCKINNEY

HH TISEVICH

LITHGOW LIBRARY
45 WINTHROP STREET

Copyright © 2019 Amanda McKinney
Names, characters and incidents depicted in this book are products of the author's imagination or are used in a fictitious manner. Any resemblance to actual events, locales, organizations, or persons, living or dead, is entirely coincidental and beyond the intent of the author or the publisher.

No part of this book may be reproduced or transmitted in any form or by any means, electronic or mechanical, including photocopying, recording, or by any information storage and retrieval system, without permission in writing from the publisher.

Paperback ISBN 978-1-7340133-4-4
eBook ISBN 978-1-7340133-3-7

Editor(s): Nancy Brown
Cover Design: Amanda Traylor

Amanda McKinney
AUTHOR OF SEXY MURDER MYSTERIES

https://www.amandamckinneyauthor.com

DEDICATION

For Mama :) :) :)

A note from the author:

Welcome to the small, southern town of Berry Springs! If you're looking for sizzling-hot alpha males, smart, independent females, and page-turning mystery, you've come to the right place. As you might have guessed, STEELE SHADOWS SECURITY is a spin-off series from the Berry Springs Series. But don't worry, you don't need to read Berry Springs first. Think of Steele Shadows as Berry Springs' darker, grittier, bad boy brother. That said, grab a tall glass of sweet tea (or vodka if you're feeling saucy), and settle in for a fun adventure that—I hope—gives you a little escape from the day to day... (and maybe a little crush on the Steele brothers).

Enjoy!

ALSO BY AMANDA MCKINNEY

NEW Thriller Series - NARRATIVE OF A MAD WOMAN:

The Widow of Weeping Pines

The Raven's Wife

The Lie Between Her (Summer 2023)

The Keeper's Closet (Summer 2023)

NEW Romantic Suspense Series - ON THE EDGE:

Buried Deception

Trail of Deception (2023)

Lethal Legacy

The Woods (A Berry Springs Novel)

The Lake (A Berry Springs Novel)

The Storm (A Berry Springs Novel)

The Fog (A Berry Springs Novel)

The Creek (A Berry Springs Novel)

The Shadow (A Berry Springs Novel)

The Cave (A Berry Springs Novel)

Devil's Gold (A Black Rose Mystery, Book 1)
Hatchet Hollow (A Black Rose Mystery, Book 2)
Tomb's Tale (A Black Rose Mystery Book 3)
Evil Eye (A Black Rose Mystery Book 4)
Sinister Secrets (A Black Rose Mystery Book 5)

BESTSELLING SERIES:

Cabin 1 (Steele Shadows Security)
Cabin 2 (Steele Shadows Security)
Cabin 3 (Steele Shadows Security)
Phoenix (Steele Shadows Rising)
Jagger (Steele Shadows Investigations)
Ryder (Steele Shadows Investigations)
Her Mercenary (Steele Shadows Mercenaries)

BESTSELLING SERIES:

Rattlesnake Road
Redemption Road

The Viper

And many more to come...

AWARDS AND RECOGNITION

JAGGER (STEELE SHADOWS INVESTIGATIONS)
2021 Daphne du Maurier Award for Excellence in Mystery/Suspense 2nd Place Winner

RATTLESNAKE ROAD
Named one of POPSUGAR's 12 Best Romance Books to Have a Spring Fling With
2022 Silver Falchion Finalist

REDEMPTION ROAD
2022 Silver Falchion Finalist

THE STORM
Winner of the 2018 Golden Leaf for Romantic Suspense
2018 Maggie Award for Excellence Finalist
2018 Silver Falchion Finalist
2018 Beverley Finalist
2018 Passionate Plume Honorable Mention Recipient

THE FOG

Winner of the 2019 Golden Quill for Romantic Suspense
Winner of the 2019 I Heart Indie Award for Romantic Suspense
2019 Maggie Award of Excellence Finalist
2019 Stiletto Award Finalist

CABIN 1 (STEELE SHADOWS SECURITY)
2020 National Readers Choice Award Finalist
2020 HOLT Medallion Finalist

THE CAVE
2020 Book Buyers Best Finalist
2020 Carla Crown Jewel Finalist

DIRTY BLONDE
2017 2nd Place Winner for It's a Mystery Contest

LET'S CONNECT!

Text **AMANDABOOKS to 66866** to sign up
for Amanda's Newsletter and get the latest
on new releases, promos, and freebies! (Don't worry, I have
no access to your phone number after you sign up.)
Or, you can sign up below.

https://www.amandamckinneyauthor.com

CABIN 3

Hidden deep in the remote mountains of Berry Springs is a private security firm where some go to escape, and others find exactly what they've been looking for.

Welcome to Cabin 1, Cabin 2, Cabin 3...

Businessman. CEO. Head of household. Three titles worst suited for Gunner Steele, the short tempered, reticent former Marine and rebel of the infamous Steele brothers. After an evening searching the mountains for his missing office manager, Gunner finds an undercover agent at his front door demanding protection—and that anyone *but him* be her bodyguard. Usually, Gunner didn't give a damn if someone disliked him, but this particular curvy vixen had information about the man who killed his father and maimed his brother. Information he'd gladly sell his soul for... but is he willing to sell hers, too?

After failure to deliver the location of a Russian spy as slippery as a bowl of borscht, Lexi York is fresh out of a job and a near-death experience when she seeks refuge at Steele Shadows, despite her disdain for the tattooed bad boy, Gunner Steele. At her wits end, Lexi devises a plan to use Gunner to get her job back, but what she hadn't planned on was developing feelings for the tortured soul she could never tame.

Unwilling to make promises he can't keep, Gunner is faced with the biggest decision of his life. Avenge his family, or throw away the only woman who's cracked open his shielded heart?

1

LEXI

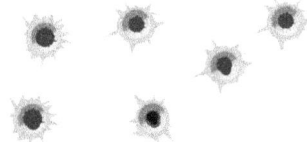

My skin burned as the binds tightened against my wrists, the hard, wooden bench I'd been laid onto no longer cold underneath my heated back. Next, large hands grabbed my ankles and secured each to the slats at the ends. My eyes squeezed shut under the black blindfold they'd wrapped around my head, an almost involuntary reaction to the terror pumping through my veins. Every contact to my body, every touch, every sensation was amped up a million percent because I couldn't see it coming. My instinct was to try to see what was happening around me but I knew if I did, the last shred of control I had would be wiped away by total darkness. They'd taken my sight, my voice, my mobility, my freedom.

I swallowed deeply, the saliva like hot sand down my throat. The sweet, metallic taste of blood seeped into my mouth from where the gag had rubbed me raw.

I inhaled through my nose. Then, exhaled, again and again, as I'd been trained to do.

Control your breathing, control your thoughts.

Control yourself.

I'd lost track of time, day, night, for every second I'd spent locked in a box no bigger than a dog cage, time had faded into some eternal black hole of neither past nor present. Just blackness.

It was the closest thing to hell I could imagine.

Just when I thought it couldn't get worse, the increased movement around me told me I was in for a rude awakening.

The room smelled old and dank. A musty scent that reminded me of the basement my sister and I used to escape and pretend we had a better life.

I zeroed in on the sounds around me. No words were spoken as my binds were checked. I'd counted two sets of boots against the concrete. One had gone still and I swear I could feel his gaze burning into me.

The one shuffling around me smelled of cigarette smoke and antiseptic, like a hospital, sending me into a horror show of scenarios that was about to happen to me.

I'd been scared before, but the fear I felt at that moment was so intense that I was sure to have a fatal heart attack if whatever these guys were about to do to me didn't kill me first.

My shoes and socks had been removed, leaving only the hospital gown they'd demanded I put on. I remember that moment vividly, the fear and panic that they were going to strip me naked. When they didn't, when they'd left the task to me, I remember being so grateful that I almost gleefully accepted being forced into a cage. They'd allowed me to keep my dignity. That "kindness" sent me into some sort of submissive state. It was a tactic, I knew that now. You've heard of Stockholm Syndrome where the victims fall in love with their captors? I could see now how that could happen. When you're in the depths of hell, with everything—

including your freedom—stripped from you, something as simple as a toothbrush becomes the greatest gift in the world, momentarily replacing fear with genuine gratitude. I felt like because they'd let me keep my clothes, I owed them.

How totally screwed up is that?

Hospital-smelling guy walked away from me. A faucet turned on.

My insides turned to water.

Quite fitting.

His footsteps coming back were like a war drum through the silence, growing nearer and nearer, bringing me closer to whatever torture they were about to inflict. Then, nothing.

Silence.

A silence so unbearable, so terrifying, that in some uncontrollable reaction, I began fighting against my binds, thrashing on the bench they'd tied me to. I bit the gag, a guttural growl coming out of me. When the skin around my wrist tore open against the binds, I stopped.

Chest heaving, I laid there, gagged and blinded, my heart a steady thumping in my ears.

I jumped at the fingertips on my face. The gag was removed, and my jaw popped open, screaming every curse word I'd ever heard from the back alleys where I grew up.

Then, it happened.

A heavy piece of fabric was placed over my nose and mouth. My entire body tensed in terror. Looking back, I actually smelled the water before it gushed over my face.

I know now why waterboarding was banned.

It is the most horrifying, indescribable mind warp that taps into a kind of panic that only few live to tell about.

When you think of torture, you probably think of pain. Let me take a second to introduce you to an entirely different kind of persecution. The kind that tortures the brain, not the body. There was very little pain involved with waterboarding. Instead, it triggered the deepest, most animalistic panic I'd ever experienced in my life. The sensation of drowning, suffocating, while being tied down has a way of breaking even the strongest-willed human. In a totally coherent state, you are gasping for air but getting none. Your lungs feeling like constricting brick walls about to cave in on each other. Every sensor piques, every voice telling you—no, *screaming* at you—that you are going to die. I felt like I was a witness to my own death. Dying, right there, dying on that bench. Totally aware of it happening to me.

You see with pain, your system releases endorphins, a natural pain and stress fighter, until eventually, you shut down. One way or another. Waterboarding is different. It is literally feeling like you are experiencing death while your mind and body are intact.

It was an experience that had haunted me every night, and every day, since.

The water stopped. The fabric was pulled away.

I spat, gagged, coughed, choking for air.

Then, again. The fabric, followed by more water, except this one lasted longer.

And this time, I vomited the moment the fabric was removed. Water and bile spewing from the depths of my empty stomach.

Again, and again it happened, allowing just enough time between each assault for me to think it was over. Until finally, I felt my conscious begin to waver, a total submission to death.

I remember my body giving up, my mind giving up, an

almost weightless sensation taking over, like I was floating up to heaven.

I was about to die. I'd given in.

"Enough."

The deep voice pulled me out of my dream-like state, like an angel granting me life. I recognized the voice instantly.

The wrap was removed from my eyes, a blinding florescent light sending a wave of nausea through me.

A large silhouette loomed over me.

"Nice work, Miss York."

"You sick, son of a—"

"Watch it. I'll take anything you've got as long as it doesn't involve my mother."

I twisted my neck to see the hospital-smelling man cutting my binds. I didn't recognize him.

The man only known as Astor, grabbed my hand and pulled me to a seated position on the bench. I looked around the room that had housed me for twenty four hours. The single light bulb above my head faded into dark corners with shelves, cages, chains, and rusty contraptions that rivaled any torture chamber. The walls were concrete, the floor, the ceiling, everything was a gray stone.

I jumped as hospital-guy reached for my wrists, his hands dry, cracked, with swollen knuckles and contorted thumbs. The guy looked like he'd seen his fair share of torture chambers.

"That's Davis," Astor said as the binds were cut. "He's the only one on payroll I've got that will do this."

I sent Hospital my most intimidating scowl—to which the corner of his lip turned up—then rubbed my wrists as I put my feet on the ground. I spat blood-tinged water, missing Astor's calf-skin Italian wing-tips by less than an inch. My aim was off.

"So." Astor casually began lowering the sleeves he'd rolled up to his elbows, as if he hadn't just ordered a woman to be tortured within an inch of her life. "That was waterboarding. A few more seconds and you would have experienced dry drowning, asphyxia, and let me tell you, that *does* hurt. Believe it or not, it could have been worse. Most victims who survive suffer damage to the lungs, permanent brain damage from lack of oxygen, and physical damage from the restraints. Not to mention the psychological damage. That reminds me..." He turned to Davis. "Call Mallory. Get an appointment set up for Miss York—"

"It's not necessary." I said.

"Yes, it is." With Astor, there was no way other than his own. He tossed me a towel and I began wiping down my face. "You did well. Are you ready for phase three of your training?"

I froze, peeking out from the towel. "Phase *three?* There's *more?*"

The wicked smirk on Astor's face had my gut clenching. At that moment, I considered running. Throwing in the proverbial towel. After all, what human would subject themselves to more?

It had been four weeks of what I can only assume was similar to special agent training at the FBI. For fourteen days, dawn until dusk, I was thrown into rigorous self-defense classes, hand-to-hand-combat and firearms training, and surveillance tactics. I was immersed in hours of foreign affair lectures worthy of a bachelor's degree. I'd lost ten pounds and had slept about the same amount in hours. Then, I'd entered phase two of training—escape and evade, otherwise known as SERE training. Little did I know this included the real-life scenario of being captured, ending with the blessed event of waterboarding.

At that point, most with half a brain would have tapped out.

Sayonara, you sick bastards.

But, you see, I was a different breed. I didn't tuck tail and run. Never had. Blame it on being raised by a single mother who was never there, or growing up in public housing in the Bronx. Whatever. I didn't care to psychoanalyze it.

The challenge had been laid down.

And I picked it up.

Astor turned and started across the basement—my cue to follow.

After sending Davis another glare—God, I hated him—I pulled on the robe I'd been tossed, and followed Astor up the rickety wooden steps. The heavy steel door opened up to a bland office hallway that gave no indication of the torture chamber below.

We rounded a corner where a group of polished twenty-somethings waited impatiently for the elevator on their cell phones. A cloud of over-priced French perfume lingered in the air, an announcement of their presence in the hallway. More like an air horn. The hot-rolled blonde, with a pitched voice that rivaled the music I'd been forced to listen to while in my cage, was demanding answers into her bejeweled cell phone about a late report. She was very important. The other, I'll call her Goldie Highlights, was texting into an oblivion, her fingers surely about to catch fire. My guess was that the texts had nothing to do with work and more to do with the Millennial she'd met at the bar the night before and how after agreeing to go home with him, she promptly retreated when things got "all too real." Both were one-hundred pounds of spin-class perfection, donning six-inch heels, designer suits and over-priced handbags. Both the living poster children for America's great entitled youth.

You should have seen their faces when I walked up.

I didn't need a mirror to tell me my eyes were as black as a raccoon's butt and as swollen as Davis's knuckles. My tangled, matted hair was sopping wet, the brown—*unhighlighted*—strings hanging over a dingy robe, loosely tied around my waist. No shoes topped off the lab rat look, complete with a disorientation in the form of unrelenting aggression.

I cocked my head and flashed a wide grin, knowing I had blood on my teeth. "Do you have any gum? I'm a little parched."

Astor groaned next to me.

Their perfectly lined eyes widened in horror, then, scanned me from head to toe in a way that took me back to the sixth-grade lunchroom. Then, with cocked brows, they dismissed me and refocused on their phones.

I didn't like being dismissed.

So I did what any temperamental toddler who'd just been waterboarded would do and slapped the phone out of Highlight's hand, sending it clamoring on the floor.

"Hey!"

The elevator dinged. I winked at my two new best friends, then followed Astor inside.

Fine, I was dragged in.

To no one's surprise, the girls waited on the next.

"I'm going to chock that up to low blood sugar, Miss York."

"I hope those aren't your next recruits."

"You'll have to work with all personalities as an agent with my company. If that's something you can't handle..."

He pressed a button and the elevator screeched to a halt. The doors slid open. "There's the exit."

I took a silent deep breath reminding myself that this was the last stepping stone to my goal.

My life's goal.

"Miss York?"

"Proceed."

The doors slid closed and we were zipped up to the top floor where the sunlight from sweeping windows spilled into the hallway like warm butter. The city of New York gleamed below us, its glittering energy palpable even from fifty floors up.

I loved the city.

I was led down a hall that smelled like fresh flowers and into a corner office walled with windows. If God had an office, this was it.

And some people thought Astor was God.

"Food and water over there." He jerked his chin to the corner. "Eat."

My jaw dropped as I walked to the garden of Eden, a white linen-covered table topped with platters of fresh fruit, vegetables, shrimp cocktail, hummus, and just about every Keto-friendly food known to man. Ice-cold water and coffee completed the spread.

Coffee.

As I piled my plate, I skimmed the office, still cagey from "phase two." Astor checked emails behind his spotless, massive oak desk that sat next to a sculpture that I was sure cost a year's worth of my salary. Also, mildly inappropriate for an office setting.

Popping grapes like M&M's, I carried my loot to a seating area complete with brown leather sofas over a spotless Chinese rug.

Astor picked up a remote and a flat screen dropped down from the ceiling, in front of a walled bookshelf filled with leather-bound books that I had no doubt Astor had read cover to cover.

A grainy black and white surveillance image popped on the screen.

"Who's that?" I asked, a piece of shrimp flying out of my mouth onto the floor.

Astor pretended not to notice. "Sergei Orlov, aka, Bear."

I washed down the shrimp with a swig of coffee—FYI, a combination I don't recommend.

"Bear?"

"A nickname that he's almost exclusively known by. Bear was born and raised in the United States by a Russian immigrant and a white-collar heiress to a coal mining fortune. He grew up with a silver spoon in his mouth, and became quite the ladies' man as he got older. After inheriting his family's fortune, Bear started Eagle Technologies, a small tech company that exploded during the internet boom. Over the next decade, Bear doubled his net worth, as well as his ego." He clicked to an image of a bloodied man lying in an alley. "This is one of his associates." He switched to another image of a man lying in bed, his body beaten to a pulp, a bullet between his eyes. "And this is a childhood friend."

"Both murdered?"

"Yes. Both cold cases."

"And you suspect it's Bear."

"I don't. The US government does."

Another blurred image filled the screen with Bear and another man, flanked by two bodyguards holding AK 47's.

"That's Andrei Sokolov, a high ranking member of the Russian SVR—formerly the KGB—who was an advocate for stronger Russian-US relations. Sokolov was assassinated in his bed by a small group of Russians who we believe have embedded themselves into our society and are actively working for the Russian government."

"You're talking about spies? Foreign espionage?"

"Exactly."

"You said a small group? How many?"

"We're not sure. The information the government provided me was very limited."

I shoveled hummus into my mouth like a backhoe. "We know Bear's one of them?"

Astor turned, his six-foot-three presence towering over me. "That's what you're going to find out."

My eyebrows popped up. Surely I wasn't hearing him—

"Phase three of your training is to go undercover as an office assistant at his tech company and monitor his every move, providing me with actionable intel on a weekly basis."

With an audible gulp, the hummus slid down my throat like a bowling ball.

"Undercover?" I cleared my throat.

"That's right. Eagle Technologies is based in Dallas, Texas, where you'll reside as a former school teacher looking to start over after a nasty divorce with her husband."

I blinked.

"You will monitor Bear from a distance, get to know his colleagues and associates. Never get too close. Is that understood?"

I nodded, a million little incoherent questions racing through my brain.

Astor crossed his arms over his chest and stared down at me. "You're tough, Miss York. Your mother would have been proud. But I only hire the best. The success of my company depends on it. Which is why a full-time position with me depends on this last part of your training. If you succeed at bringing me actionable intel, phase three will be complete and we will discuss your future as an agent within my company."

Goosebumps prickled my arms. The end of the tunnel. The end of ten years of working tirelessly toward my goal of becoming a special agent with Astor Stone, Inc.

"I suggest you go home, recoup. Pack only what you need. You leave in forty-eight hours."

"Two days?"

"Is that a problem?"

"Uh. No sir."

"Good." He walked to his desk. "This should be a quick and painless assignment. Remember, your goal is only to *observe* Bear, nothing else."

I could do quick and painless... but something in my gut told me nothing about infiltrating a Russian espionage ring was going to be quick.

Or painless.

"You'll receive a visit from my assistant tomorrow where she'll provide you everything you need for your cover, including a detailed background story. You are to know it forward and backwards. You will no longer be Lexi York. You become your cover, understand? You are to remain unimpressionable, at best. People need to like you, then forget you the moment you walk away."

I'd like to think that part was going to be a challenge but truth was, over the last few years, I'd become as boring as a dinner napkin. One of those plain white ones, not the delicate, ornate doilies. Lord knew there was nothing delicate about me. Despite my best efforts.

"Also, if you expect to be an agent with my company, you'll need to have that tattoo removed from your arm."

"My... But—"

"There's no but. It's as good as gone."

Shrimp in hand, I ran my knuckles over my arm.

His phone rang.

I decided to take an exit before he told me I had to cut off my hair. I grabbed my coffee and plate—because no way in hell I was leaving that goldmine—and stood.

"To be clear, Miss York. If you fail, you're out."

"Out?"

"Out of a job. You fail, therefore, you will no longer work at my company."

I blinked, my excitement dissolved by the pressure that just settled on my shoulders.

Then, it got heavier.

"I want to make it clear, Miss York, if your cover is blown, Astor Stone will deny having any knowledge of your visit to Texas. There will be no cavalry coming over the hill for you." He nodded to the exit—

"That'll be all."

2

LEXI

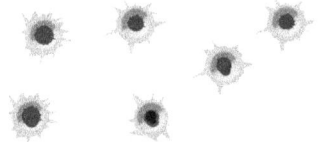

Six months later...

"*Earth to Lexi.*"

I blinked, snapping my gaze away from the black ocean swirling below me.

"What?"

"I said, *earth to Lexi.*" Kara, my double-D cup, mildly promiscuous, mimosas-for-breakfast, curves-for-days, bestie leaned forward. Her tattooed breasts swelling up to her neck, her neon-blue drink sloshing on the table. I was surprised the iron didn't disintegrate on contact.

"Sorry," I muttered, shifting in my seat.

"*Girl.* We're in one of the hottest bars in Aruba sitting under a full moon next to the freaking ocean. It's seventy-eight degrees outside. You can't toss a cherry"—she flicked the one I'd plucked from my drink—"without hitting a walking orgasm everywhere you look."

My brow arched. I'd missed an orgasm? It certainly wouldn't be the first time.

I released the grip from my drink, each finger peeling away from the stem where the sugar had melted like glue. Sugar, pure grain alcohol and something else that I was pretty sure was going to put a hole in my liver by morning.

Kara continued, "It's the first time we've been together in six months since you left New York. You denied those tequila shots from the guys across the bar. You haven't even touched your drink. Don't tell me you lost your edge in Texas."

A long, slow exhale punctuated the restless irritation vibrating through me. I plucked her melted drink off the table and downed half the thing like it was a bottle of formula. This earning me a few *whoots* from the table next to us and an instant brain freeze that felt like knives piercing my temples. Note to self to never chug a drink named the "panty dropper,"—or any drink on special for ninety-nine cents. Shocker, by the way.

"Heeeey..." Scowling, Kara grabbed the drink.

"You know better than to challenge my drinking abilities."

"Or, her *edginess*." This from Bev, my overly-conservative heiress to a plumbing fortune bestie. "I had to pull her away from the tattoo place downtown." She looked at me. "Kara's right. What's up with you?"

My brain kickstarted into change-subject mode. "Sorry," I looked at Kara. "I was just mentally counting off how much you owe me after that little stunt you pulled downtown."

"I thought he was selling potpourri!"

"Sure you did. Where did that stuff go, anyway?"

A wicked smile crossed Kara's face.

"Ah, so that's what happened to the leftover pizza and ice

cream. Must've been some potent potpourri." I winked, then tilted my head to the side. "And by the way, next time a seven foot stranger dressed in black lures you into an alley to buy some *potpourri*, don't come crying to me for cash."

"Fine. And by the way, you could use some potpourri yourself. You need to snap out of whatever it is you're thinking about, *grandma,* because if you don't, I'm about to go talk to that sex-on-a-stick surfer that's been eyeing you since we got here."

I straightened and fought the urge to steal a glance at the so-called sex-stick behind me. Instead, I focused on my two best friends, Bev and Kara, who were the entire reason I was there. They were right, I needed to loosen up.

Potpourri or not.

I took a quick sip of the bubble-gum pink concoction they called a 'Flaming Flamingo.' "I'm sorry, guys. Really, I've just been—"

"Thinking about work, we know." Bev sipped her very appropriate gin and tonic.

Kara leaned in. "You know, you're never gonna work your way up at that private investigation firm if you burn out by age thirty-five."

"She's right, Lex. You're going to work yourself into the ground. We're just saying, try not to think about it every *second* of your life."

Kara yanked a few napkins from the dispenser, deciding to dab up her toxic puddle from the table. "And isn't that why we're here? Get away from everything for a bit? That includes work *and* exes." She glanced at me and winked. "Which shouldn't be hard for you, Lex."

"And impossible for you since you got the last guy's name tattooed on your ass. What is it again? Oh, that's right, *Bobby*. Bobby right there on your butt cheek. Butt-cheek Bobby. No six hour plane ride is scrubbing that thing off."

Bev burst out laughing as Kara sent me her best scowl. I forced a grin, although I knew that if I had one more drink, I might very well pick a fight with someone simply to funnel the anxiety spinning inside me.

Maybe I needed some of that potpourri after all.

Most people who'd recently lost everything that meant anything to them usually did.

My story went something like this.

Ten years ago I'd accepted a position as a research tech at Astor Stone, an up-and-coming New York based private investigations company.

Or so I thought.

It wasn't long before I realized Astor Stone was a heck of a lot more than tracking cheating spouses, proving insurance fraud, and finding Mrs. Bertha's lost cat. No, those kinds of clients didn't arrive in blacked-out Escalades with five-person security detail. It took months of snooping, listening to conversations through vents, and one date with the red-headed IT manager—still wasn't proud of that one —to learn that the company I worked for was secretly contracted with the US government to research and vet out potential threats before an official assessment was opened for whatever, or whoever, they'd asked us to investigate. Red-headed IT guy had sworn me to secrecy, to which I demanded the same in return for our little roll in the hay. Side note: systematic thinkers really do overanalyze things in the bedroom. It was a game of Tetris with him trying to figure out how things fit. Regardless of the poking and prodding, IT guy had given me a new dream to chase. Becoming a special agent with Astor Stone replaced my old dream of working for the FBI. Fewer boundaries, less red tape, more money. A lot more. So, I'd put my nose to the grindstone, working twelve hour days, spending my time buried in endless paperwork, working in a position that was as boring as standing in line at the post office.

Unless you had a book on your phone, of course. A *really* good one. With lots of sex.

The dirty kind.

Anyway, I'd kept telling myself that after I was promoted to an agent—I'd slow down. Take awesome vacations. Take time to myself when I could. Maybe even get a man that involved more than a 'thanks for a great night.' *Night*, as in, *singular*.

Months stretched to years, years stretched to a decade. That's right, a decade. I knew Astor Stone inside and out, although no one realized I did. But the hours and dedication I'd put in weren't getting me recognized by the executive team. So, I'd decided to take matters into my own hands. On my thirtieth birthday, I put on my tightest pair of Spanx paired with a bra that had more padding than butt lifting panties, and walked straight into the CEO's office—a former black ops jarhead known only as Astor—and told him I knew what his company did and I wanted to be considered for the next agent position.

The next day, I'd arrived to work with a sticky note on my computer that read—

12 floor, Rm 1207

I didn't even know Astor had offices on the twelfth floor of the New York high-rise.

That's how it all began. And this was how it ended.

I'd arrived in Texas with one carry-on bag, a new identity, and a key to my new apartment, where I was to report to Eagle Technologies to begin my first undercover assignment.

Succeed or fail.

Fail and I was out of a job.

They say New Yorkers are a particularly impatient breed of people. This stereotype was proven to be true when the days turned into weeks... and weeks turned into months.

Months *and months*.

Eight to five, five days a week of *"Eagle Technologies, how may I direct your call? Please hold."* One hundred and eighty-three days of a mind-numbingly boring existence sitting behind a chintzy desk and taking calls on a phone that always smelled like a steaming bowl of borscht. One-hundred and eighty-three days living in a seedy, one bedroom apartment to fit the cover of a newly-divorced former school teacher looking for a fresh start and new life.

It was enough to drive anyone insane.

Not this gal.

For every bottle of cheap hair dye and fake giggles behind the phone, my resolve to expose the Russian spy known as Bear became stronger. Tireless.

Relentless.

I was committed because I had to be. Because my job, my dream, depended on it.

I filled my evenings by enrolling in a mixed martial arts class and joining the local shooting range—two very appropriate ways to spend a Monday evening in the South, I learned. Throw in a can of Aqua Net and drinks at the local honky tonk bar, and all of a sudden, my cell phone started recognizing y'all as an autocorrect.

Days blended together, each weekly report to Astor

providing barely enough intel to keep me employed. It wasn't easy. I had to scrape the bottom of the barrel to get what little information I could find on the guy. Bear, on all counts, was a hard-working stand-up citizen with two cats and a penchant for charitable donations. The opposite of what you'd expect with a Russian spy. Boring, on all counts.

Until the day that everything got flipped on its head.

One Monday morning, Bear didn't show to work. Same for the next day, and the next. The guy was suddenly MIA. Gone. No one had heard from him, no one knew where he was. It was as if the Russian had vanished into thin air.

Astor didn't like this very much and was quick to let me know that I should have seen it coming. Should have been tailing him. I should have known where the guy ran off to.

And so, my undercover position took a shift. My promotion was no longer contingent on actionable intel, it was contingent upon me finding the suspected Russian spy. I was given two weeks. Two weeks to track down the man the government suspected of foreign espionage, or lose my job.

At 5:01pm on the fourteenth day I was fired from Astor Stone. Reason? Failure to deliver Sergei Orlov's, aka Bear's, location.

At 3:31pm the following day, I bought a last minute airplane ticket to join my two best friends on their pre-arranged girls' trip to Aruba.

I had no job, no money, the home and car I'd had while undercover now belonged to Astor Stone, Inc. I was sitting in a really screwed up mental purgatory between the cover I'd been living for months, and the real Lexi York. As if I needed anything else to make me feel more lost.

Of course I didn't tell Kara or Bev any of this. My best friends didn't know about my undercover gig. I'd told them I'd simply been transferred to Texas. They had no clue I'd just been fired from the only real job I'd ever had. Ten years of my life down the drain. My dreams down the drain.

I didn't even have a place to go when I got back.

That girls' trip was my last hurrah before I spent the next months of my life picking up the broken pieces and searching for a new job.

Back to square one.

Totally, one-hundred percent starting over.

And to top it all off, the trip wasn't exactly the hurrah I'd expected.

When I agreed to the "girls' vacation," I had mornings at the spa, afternoons with books—lots of books—and evening meditation in mind. What I got was day drinking, night clubbing, and trolling for men every second in between. Don't get me wrong, I like to have a good time. I like men, I like drinking. I've been known to cut a rug a time or two. Believe me, I've had plenty of wild, late nights. One time involving seven shots of tequila and a game of five finger fillet that ended with a late night visit to the ER. Last I heard, my ex still didn't have feeling in his last two fingers. Or any pride left, for that matter. Lately, though, most of my evenings involved a box of wine, a stack of books, and a wicked crick in my neck the next day from reading all night.

Truth was I *was* a workaholic. Somewhere over the last ten years I'd turned into my mom.

God, I missed her.

And now, all that was over.

Hard to be a workaholic when you didn't have a job.

I looked down at the melted ice in my drink and realized I'd only taken two sips.

Dammit, Lexi, loosen up, I scolded myself. *For one freaking night, loosen up.*

My hand shot up at the waitress sauntering by. "Excuse

me ma'am?" I pretended not to notice Kara and Bev mock my *ma'am*.

"What can I get for ya?"

"Three shots of whiskey. Chivas Regal."

"ID?"

I pulled my passport from my purse, although based on the amount of pre-teens I'd seen in the place, I assumed an old Blockbuster card would have sufficed.

"Be right back." The waitress strode away.

Kara and Bev pounced.

"Ooooooohhhhh...." Kara wiggled her eyebrows.

"Whiskey?" Bev wrinkled her pointy nose. "You've been in the south too long."

The girl had no freaking idea.

"Who cares? Shots. *That's* our girl." Kara clapped her hands. "Welcome back, Lex."

I smiled, inhaled and... felt good. Real good. *Engage, Lexi, be present.* I shoved my phone into my purse—the phone I always kept on in case work called—and took a moment to soak in the view. Thanks to Kara's hypnotic flirting, we were in the VIP section of the most popular tiki bar on the strip, packed to the gills with girls wearing scraps of clothing that no one in their right mind would consider an outfit—and every man would approve of. To my right, an endless ocean as black as coal sparkling under the moon. Two twinkling cruise ships sat on the horizon. The weather was warm, drinks were tolerable. The men *were* sizzling hot. Kara was right, Aruba was paradise.

"Ladies, here're your shots."

I raised my shot. "To leaving work and the dirty south behind."

Kara nodded. "And maybe picking up one of those tattoo-guys in the corner."

My gaze shifted to the four tanned, muscular twenty-somethings winking at us.

Not bad. Not bad at all.

"Bottom's up." I threw back the shot, welcoming the burn.

Work time over, play time begin.

Two more rounds later the bar was hopping. I mean, literally hopping. The bass from the music felt like drumsticks pounding the sides of my head. The tattoo guys had found their way to our table—seconds after our third round of shots. Funny, the timing there. Dax, as he'd demanded I called him, had cuddled up to me and was in the middle of telling me how much he liked *my eyes* when a pair of drunk cowboys bumped into our table, spilling Dax's drink all over me.

The guy didn't even flinch.

"Excuse me," I said when the inebriated jerk didn't move.

"Sorry, I can, uh, get you—"

"It's fine."

I grabbed my purse and squeezed between the chairs—directly into Cowboy's hand sliding up my skirt, all the way up to my thong.

And that was it.

That was my breaking point.

Memories of my sister and I walking to school alongside gang members and overdosers flashed through my head. That one time—that *one* time—my sister was pulled into an alley. If I had to bet, that guy's right nut was still lodged in his throat.

I saw red.

I grabbed Cowboy's hand, spun on my heel, twisted, and slammed the drunk bastard's head on the table. Gritting my teeth, I leaned over him, pressing my chest against his back and whispered in his ear, "You ever touch me, or one of my girls like that again, you're going to need more than a doctor to straighten out your wrist. Got me?"

By this time, a crowd had gathered, along with a security guard who hauled the bastard away.

I turned to the girls, whose eyes were the size of our waitress's breasts.

I cleared my throat and smoothed my skirt. "And you guys thought I lost my edge."

"Where did you learn to fight like that?"

My stomach dipped. I forced a wink, then nodded to the spilled liquor all over my clothes. "I'll be back."

Tattoo dude number one wrapped his arms around Kara. "Don't worry, we'll keep your friends safe."

Midnight chivalry at its best.

Feeling all sorts of pissed-off and jittery now, I pushed my way through the sea of drunks to the flickering sign that read *"athrooms."*

I blew out a breath as I stopped. The line to the single-stall *athroom* was seven, maybe eight girls—and one non-binary—deep. There was no way I was waiting for that line to clear. It was a new skirt, after all.

"Uhhh, there's somes bathrooms the next building overs on the third floor," a girl—couldn't have been a day over sixteen—slurred in my ear. She nodded toward a newly-constructed building with reflective siding, long glass windows, and two balconies where people mingled next to a band.

Now *that* was my kind of party.

"Thanks." I leaned in. "And you've got a nipple showing."

I found my way through the exit to a breezeway connecting the buildings. As the *thud, thud, thud* of the bass faded behind me, I felt my pulse begin to calm. I slowed my pace, closed my eyes and took a deep breath, savoring the silence. With a stupid smile on my face, I walked into the shiny new building, complete with marble floors and dim golden lights perfect for selfies. A low, relaxing melody floated through the air. Very, very nice. I made my way up to the third floor and found a sign that included all letters of the word *Bathroom*.

Things were already looking up.

Or so I thought.

3

GUNNER

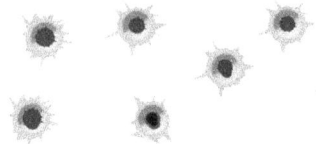

A cold, wet mist clung to the air like a blanket, the narrow beam of my flashlight fading into the shifting cloud of drops around me. As if I needed anything else to hamper the shit visibility I already had. The moonless night was as black as a bat's ass and temperatures had dipped into the mid-forties.

Gotta love autumn in the south.

It wasn't my first time sneaking through the woods at night. First as a defiant, bullheaded little pissant in my youth, then, years later, as a defiant bullheaded special ops Marine. Over the years, I'd learned two things about a moonless night. One, never assume you're alone. Two, use your other senses as a guide.

I'd ripped off my gloves and jacket sometime after the last creek I'd splashed through, letting the air around me, the wind, the moisture, the raw nature guide me with each step.

It had been over an hour since the incessant chatter of the search party behind me had faded into the wind. The small-town "do-gooders" were gone, the light was gone, the day was gone. Even the dogs had left me alone... which tended to happen when you yelled at their handlers. That was nothing compared to the rant I'd unleashed on a balding former beat cop—who'd only joined the party for the free coffee and donuts—when he'd suggested we call it a night.

Call it a night.

Not on my fucking life.

It had been twenty-seven hours since Celeste Russo—office manager of Steele Shadows Security—had gone missing. Twenty-seven hours since my younger brother Axel had found her front door unlocked and blood splatter all over her living room.

Twenty-seven hours of tireless searching, looking for the woman we all considered a sister.

I'd arranged a search party within an hour of her disappearance, rounding up as many Steele Shadows employees and former military guys as I could find—most, one and the same. Over the course of the day, word had gotten out and the whole town had shown up, causing irritation to mix with my already amped-up urgent state. While my buddies knew what to look for, and as importantly, what to look *out* for, the well-meaning rednecks of Berry Springs had no clue what they were doing. Each hellbent on trampling any tracks or evidence that could lead us to Celeste's abductor.

Assuming she was taken, of course.

It was the shit show of all shit shows and had ended with me telling the mayor to go fuck himself, which, by the way, wasn't the first time I'd done that. I mentioned something about my defiant youth, didn't I?

Ax took lead on arranging the SAR teams, a show of leadership that didn't go unnoticed by me, or everyone else.

Yeah, I'd caught their glances, seen their looks, waiting on bated breath and nimble toes to see how I'd react.

A wary curiosity with just enough doubt to spread like wildfire.

It was a look I'd gotten all my life.

The delinquent Steele brother... but never say it to his face.

So, as usual, I'd broken away from the search party and taken off on my own, figuring I could cover three times as much ground as the glorified ambulance chasers who were only here for the gossip.

"Oh you were there? Tell me..." I could hear the chatter at Donny's Diner the next morning. Hyper gossip behind fresh flapjacks and hot coffee while my brothers and I were still on the hunt. Because, by my estimate, by the time the sun rose, we would've covered only a quarter of the vast mountain range that surrounded Celeste's cabin.

Jagged cliffs, steep ravines, creeks, rivers, caves. A million places to hide. A million places for inexperienced asswipes to break a neck. Not that I'd wish that on anyone. Ankle, maybe. Neck, probably not.

Probably not.

I'd just stepped off a rotted log that crossed one of those very steep ravines, when I stopped. Froze like a statue in the inky mist swirling around me.

Call it a finely tuned instinct from over a decade running black ops, but something told me I wasn't alone. In those mountains, that could be anything from a four-hundred pound grizzly bear, to a tweaked-out camper with a hefty case of paranoia and a rusty knife.

My focus shifted to a twig popping behind me. I switched off my flashlight and the world went dark. It was as if someone had wrapped a black bag over my head. An experience I don't recommend. Trust me.

Unlike my brothers—or most people, probably—I bypassed the SIG on my hip and went for the KA-BAR tucked in my boot. There wasn't a target I couldn't shoot, moving, still, hundreds of yards away, inches from my face. At some point, that lack of challenge had inspired me to pick up a knife and train myself how to become as deadly with a blade as a gun. Before long, my knife became an extension of my arm. I'll be dammed if I didn't love the brutality of it. Something about hand to hand combat. Strength against strength. Will against will.

The intimacy of it.

The savagery of it.

May the best man win.

And I always fucking won.

I felt that cool tingle in my balls as my body prepared to meet whatever was stalking me. After the last few weeks, I welcomed an assault with open arms. I was more than ready to send my fist, nose, blade, whatever, into something or someone else.

The breeze halted, the woods around me went silent as my grip tightened around the knife.

Then, the slightest *snick* right behind me.

Here we go.

I closed my eyes... inhaled... then spun on my heel and lunged through the underbrush. Matching my speed, my stalker took off like a bullet.

I sprinted through the brush like a deer, maneuvering the rocks, limbs, tree roots with ease, a talent my brothers and I had gained at a very young age.

My first surprise was that my stalker had the same speed and agility as I did—as someone who'd trained years for it.

Branches swiped my legs, arms, and face as I blindly darted though the woods following the quick steps ahead of me. A dark silhouette soared over a fallen tree. I grabbed the limb, hurling myself over a boulder to catch up.

Surprise number two—my stalker had a heck of a vertical. We splashed through a creek, the freezing water drenching my ATAC boots and pants. Hate wet boots. I gritted my teeth and pressed on, the sound of steps growing fainter in the distance.

Was I being outrun?

I was being *outrun*?

Adrenaline burst through my veins as I pushed up a hill, using every rock as leverage to increase speed. I breached the top and stopped.

Nothing. No footsteps, no heavy breathing. Not even a faintest snick.

I clicked on my light, noticing a break in the leaves that covered the ground. I took off again, across the clearing and into the woods. Minutes passed as I jogged, listening, searching.

"Hey!" A flash of light from the side blinded me.

BAM!

My feet flew out from under me from the force of the body that just leapt out from behind a tree. We tumbled to the ground, rolling down a hill with blades for rocks. We landed with a thud against a tree trunk, nearly splitting my back in half.

I was up and straddling the bastard in seconds flat, with one hand pinning their wrists above their head and the other holding my knife to their neck.

"Whoa, *Gunner,* what the *fuck,* man? Get off me!"

"Jagg?" I released my hold and blinked through the darkness. Detective Max Jagger, dressed in a hoodie, jeans, and combat boots hurled me off of him with a few curse words I hadn't heard since the last time I'd been in jail.

I jumped to a stance. "What the hell are you doing out here?"

Jagg grabbed his light from the ground and began dusting himself off. "You think detectives sit around and jack off all fucking day? I'm doing the same thing you are, you high-strung son of a bitch—you almost killed me."

"I almost killed you? Who the fuck tackles someone in the middle of the damn woods? At night?"

"I saw the blade in your hand."

"Saw my knife? What are you, a bat?"

"Yep and if you ever put a blade to my throat again, I'll drain every ounce of your blood."

"Well, nice fucking work detective…" I glanced down the mountain. "You just let whoever was following me get away."

"Looks like he'd already gotten away from you."

The words stung like a bee. I pushed it aside.

"He?"

"Best I could tell, yeah. When I saw you two *lighting rods* sprinting through the woods, I followed. Gage told me you'd gone out this way, so I figured you were one of them. Didn't know which was which. Figured you'd have your gun so I went after the guy with the knife. Why a knife, by the way?"

"To gut people who tackle me in the middle of the woods. You get a visual?"

"Nope, nothing. Just two assholes running through the woods."

"Not even hair color, height?"

"Nope."

Suddenly, from above—

"You had him by a handful of inches."

Jagg and I twisted our necks toward the voice coming out of the maple tree next to us.

"*God*, is that you?" Jagg mocked.

"Ax?" I stepped back and angled my flashlight, the beam reflecting off the zipper of my brother's leather jacket. "What the hell are you doing up there?"

Bright orange leaves rained onto us as Ax shimmied down the tree like a damn spider monkey. Kid could climb to the top of any tree on the mountain, blindfolded with one arm tied behind his back.

He landed like a nimble fairy.

"I can see every mountain top from that view. I've been watching for lights, campfire, anything. What I got was three yahoos running like idiots through the dark."

"You see him?"

"Only that he was shorter than you. Heck of a sprinter, though."

"Everyone's shorter than you assholes." Jagg, a six-foot-two former Navy SEAL was only an inch shorter than my brothers and me... and miles insecure about it.

"Why didn't you take a shot?" I asked Ax.

"Some of us aren't as trigger happy as you are, Gunner. Who knows who it was? Could have been a spooked teenager who joined the search party and decided to follow you around."

"No shit, Gunn," Jagg chimed in. "Cool it a bit."

"You fucking cool it."

"Dude." Ax turned toward me. "You're running on empty. If you don't bring it down a notch, Dallas is going to sneak an Ambien into your PBR tonight and chain you to your bed."

"Let her practice on me first." Jagg wiggled his eyebrows.

"You get closer than three inches to our stepmother and I'll wrap your dick around your throat."

He laughed.

Ax tilted his head to the side, studying my arm. "Jagg got your new tat, bro."

I looked down at the trickle of blood running down my arm, sure enough coming from the center of the eagle I'd recently had inked on my forearm. The final tattoo enclosing the sleeve down to my wrist would now forever have a lightning bolt-shaped scar between its legs.

Fan*ta*stic.

Jagg grinned. "Hey, at least it's a few inches."

"Yeah, matches yours."

"I'll have Snake touch it up and send me the bill."

"Damn right you will."

"Anyway," Ax looked back and forth between Jagg and I. "What's new? What have I missed? Anything?"

I shook my head and took a step back, wanting nothing more than to punch a tree trunk. Maybe Ax was right, maybe I needed a second of sleep. Maybe even a whole sixty minutes.

Jagg picked a spider web out of his hair. "Got an update from Celeste's cell phone carrier that I should have her records first thing this morning."

"You won't find anything." Ax said.

"Why? Because your super-genius security guy Wolf has already hacked into her records?"

Silence.

"Fine. What will I *not* see?"

"Celeste received no texts or calls from anyone other than us on the night she disappeared. Aside from a few spam calls, same thing for the days leading up." Ax flickered me a glance. "Celeste wasn't nearly as social as we thought she was."

Or, as open with us as we'd thought. During our canvass of her house, we'd learned that Celeste's parents "who'd moved to Europe after she'd joined the military," were actually deceased, passing away two months short of Celeste's eighteenth birthday. We also learned that the tattooed southern tomboy who could almost outshoot me—*almost*—was an avid knitter whose bedroom television had been left on the Hallmark Channel. There was a shockingly feminine side to Celeste that no one knew about. A bit discerning, sure. But bottom line, Celeste was a former Marine who'd take a bullet for any one of us. The pink doilies didn't matter. Her loyalty did. My brothers and I were going to go to the ends of the earth to find out what had happened to her.

"Something doesn't feel right about it." Jagg shook his head. "Celeste was someone who could handle her own. I wrestled her in the ring once and about lost my ass. Don't mind admitting it because I got a few nice shots of hers. Like two candy apples it was. Anyway, what I'm saying is—the girl knew security. She knew how to be safe. She wasn't stupid. By all accounts, it appears that she simply went home last night and had some sort of struggle with someone, and then *bam,* is gone. It wasn't a robbery gone wrong. Everything's still at her place; the only thing missing is her."

"You're right that Celeste could handle her own. She could handle anyone in a fight—"

"Unless she was incapacitated," I said.

"What do you mean?" Ax asked. "Chloroform?"

"Sure. Anything."

"Two scenarios, then: She was either knocked out and taken, or threatened and went willingly."

"With someone she knows." I added. It was something that had been twisting my gut from hour one.

"We don't know that for sure right now, Gunner."

"Come on, Jagg. You said yourself there wasn't a break-in. Gage, the local PD, and you *all* verified that. Celeste wouldn't leave her doors unlocked. Someone went to her house, and she let them in. Whoever that person is, has her now."

"Was she dating anyone?" Ax asked. "I remember her saying something about a bad date recently."

"Already checked into him." Jagg said. "He's got an alibi, and is a pansy-ass brat if you ask me. Not even her type."

"How do you know who her last date was with?"

Jagg cocked his head. "Why do I always have to remind you that I'm a detective? That I investigate for a living? I asked Dallas. She told me."

"What do you mean you asked Dallas?"

"I asked her about Celeste's personal life, her love life, or whatever you call it. I guess they're pretty close."

"Girl talk," Ax muttered.

We wrinkled our noses.

"I still don't understand how there's not a trace. Not a single trace of her anywhere."

"It's like she vanished into thin air."

A light breeze swept through the trees. We watched a bright red leaf drift to the ground.

Where the hell was Celeste?

"Alright, guys." Ax clicked on his flashlight. "Let's head down the mountain. Dallas set up a secondary rendezvous site by the creek."

We fell into step together, descending into the woods.

Jagg checked his phone, then slid it back into his pocket. "Dallas also told me that Celeste seemed a bit off lately. You guys see that?"

Our lack of response had Jagg narrowing his eyes. "Guys. Did Celeste seem off to you?"

"I mean..." Ax cleared his throat. "Normal, I guess."

"Yeah," I said. "Normal."

He laughed. "You don't even really know her, do you? You look at her like she's a guy, don't you? Don't pay attention to her moods, shit like that..."

"Nice of you to show up, Phil. You lose your ballsac back there?"

"Dr. Phil, you idiot. And it doesn't take a daytime self-help show to know that women talk about stuff. Need to. You want to get to know a woman, talk to her friends, or better yet, her sister if she has one. Women talk. They pick up on things, trust me."

"This from the guy who took his last date to Chubby's BBQ after the demolition derby."

"Hey. We had VIP seats."

"Next to the porta potties."

"Exactly. Doesn't get more VIP than that. Besides, at least I've had a date." An elbow slammed into my side. "I've been thinking you've switched sides lately, Gunner."

I raised my knife. "Come here, Jagg, let me show you which side I prefer—"

"Enough." Ax sent a fist into my shoulder. "You need to freaking eat something, dude."

"You think Dallas has food?" Jagg asked.

"Dallas always has food."

"Cupcakes?"

"What are you, six? Yes. I'm sure she has every baked good known to man."

"Whiskey?"

My brother and I looked at Jagg as if he'd sprouted wings.

"Sorry, forgot who I was with. Well hell yeah, then, I could use a drink after getting a knife shoved to my throat."

"When did you become such a bitch, Jagg?"

"When have you ever *not* been a hot-headed, bulldozing, stubborn son of a bitch, Gunn?"

"Sociability was never one of my brother's strong suits." Ax winked.

"Or tolerance. Or patience." Jagg added.

"Fuck you."

After that debilitating comeback—and a few more chuckles from Jagg—we took off down the mountain in silence.

"My babies."

I stepped out of the tree line to a beaming smile and open arms.

"Hey, ma." After a hug and peck on the cheek, our stepmother moved on to Ax while I took a moment to soak in the scene.

A pair of blinding headlights illuminated at least a dozen people—half in cowboy hats and Carhartt's—huddled around two folding tables flanked by portable heaters. Dead leaves covered the riverbank, next to a calm river, a contradiction to the undercurrent of drama in the air. Steam puffed from the mouths of the gossips and swirled from the piping hot coffee Dallas had served up. The annoying, low buzz of chatter broke the silence of nature.

A pair of freezing fingertips grabbed my chin.

"Gunner, you look terrible. You need to eat. After that, you need to sleep."

I forced a smile as I looked down at my stepmom in her furry winter hat, couture down jacket that hung to her knees, and hiking boots fresh from the box. Not that it was her first time in hiking boots. Dallas knew her way around the woods, she just bought a new pair after every hike. Scuffed shoes were blasphemous in her spotless walk-in two-room closet. The only thing that outnumbered her shoes? Her bags—purses, handbags, whatever they were called.

Wasted money is what they should be called.

"Come, eat." She repeated.

"I'm good, ma. Is Gage still at the hospital with Feen?"

She nodded, her face dropping.

"Who's on shift next?"

"Supposed to be you, but I want you to go home and rest. You're running yourself thin, Gunner. Like always."

"I'm fine. I'll head to the hospital after I leave here."

"Fine; I know better than to argue with you. But you won't leave here until you get some food in your system. Oh, and, uh," she leaned in. "Leslie's here."

I didn't bother to hide my groan. "The bar let her out early, huh?"

"Stop that, Gunner. Bartender or not, a job's a job and to be respected. She's a nice girl."

I shot Dallas a look, to which she rolled her eyes.

"You've got to give someone a chance, son. Come on."

With every expletive known to man shooting through my head like flaming cannon balls, I was dragged to the tables where the chatter hushed and all attention turned to me—the unofficial CEO of Steele Shadows Security. A title that had been bestowed upon me now that Dad was gone and Feen was fighting for his life in the ICU.

A CEO.

CE-*fucking*-O.

Jesus. *Christ.*

He'll never make it, the looks said. *Jarheads like him can't run a business.* Or, my all-time favorite—*no one will invest in anything he touches with a rap sheet like that.*

Bastards.

I stepped up to the table. True to form, Dallas had endless boxes of muffins, cupcakes, actual cakes, and carafes of coffee. Half gluten and dairy free, half with flax and something called chia hidden in the frosting. Dallas was nothing if not predictable.

Standing at the edge of the table with her gloved hands around a Styrofoam cup was Leslie Ambrose. Her long, blonde hair blowing in the wind, exposing the wings of an angel tattooed on her neck.

I stifled a snort.

"Hey there, Gunner," she smiled that feline smile as Dallas began filling two plates to the rim.

Now, I've been known to have more than my fair share of booze and also been known to hide it well. I've also been known to detect it like a damn breathalyzer on others. Right then, my 0.08% radar was going off like crazy. Leslie stumbled on her red combat boots, complete with hot pink lacings.

"Hey," I eyed her as one might a rabid dog.

"You've been out here all night?"

"You've been out here five minutes?" Always an asshole, or so I'd been told. Unintended... half the time anyway.

"What? Girls can't participate in search and rescues, Gunner?"

"Didn't say that."

"Well wouldn't surprise me if you did, you know. You never were as smooth as your brothers."

"Thanks."

"You're welcome," she quipped back and had me instantly hating the conversation.

I watched her sway a bit as she sipped, wondering what I'd been thinking with her. I wasn't thinking with my head, that's for damn sure—the one that sits on my shoulders, anyway.

She tilted her head and searched my face like someone might dissect an algebraic equation. One of those really hard ones.

"You feelin' okay?"

Jesus.

I grabbed the first thing I could find on the table, which happened to be a vegan carrot something. "Fine."

"You don't look fine."

I would have given my inheritance to the Devil himself for the ground to open up and suck me under. I shot a glance at an eavesdropping Dallas who snapped her gaze away.

"Talking to you's like pulling teeth, you know that?" Leslie continued.

My gaze shifted to Ax and Jagg. Ax, face buried in his cell phone, and Jagg wiggling his eyebrows and chuckling his ass off.

Should've knifed him when I had a chance.

"Whatever, Gunner. You're obviously not fine. Everyone's talking about it."

I tossed my carrot thing on the table. It bounced like a plastic ball, catching the attention of the few cowboys huddled by the corner.

Were baked goods supposed to bounce?

In nothing short of a shocking move, drunk angel caught it mid-air and took a bite. "Not bad. Better than what I've got at home."

A little lightbulb went off. "You live around the mountain, right?"

Her brow lifted. "Uh, *yeah*. Don't remember?"

Six shots of tequila and four beers didn't lend itself to much of a memory. But that was the least of my worries at that moment. Leslie lived two country miles from Celeste.

"Were you home last night?"

She thought for a very long moment. "Yeah, I was."

"Do you remember seeing anyone drive by? Late at night?"

Dallas slid two plates in front of me, then slinked away.

"Uhhh... Come to think of it, I remember hearing a loud engine sometime after midnight."

"What kind of vehicle? Could you tell?"

"I didn't see it. I remember it was loud."

"Truck?"

"No, louder."

"A motorcycle?"

She nodded slowly. "Yeah, yeah, that sounds about right."

A motorcycle would've been Ax driving to Celeste's to check on her. Damn.

Leslie's swirly eyes drifted to the woods and slanted with concern. "I can't believe she's missing. One of our own."

One of *our* own, I thought. I picked up my plate and shoved a piece of zucchini bread in my mouth. "Well, good to see ya," I muttered around bites. As I turned, she called out.

"Wait. Gunner? I think I remember hearing a second motorcycle last night."

I stopped and swallowed—the zucchini whatever like a damn cotton ball sliding down my throat. "What time?"

"Around the same time as the other."

"So you heard two bikes last night?"

"Yeah, I guess I did. They were about forty minutes apart."

I blinked.

"Anyway," she stepped closer, enough for me to smell the liquor on her breath. Whiskey. Definitely whiskey. A lopsided smile cracked her makeup. "Want to get out of here? Go see if whoever it was drives by again?"

I looked her up and down, part of me considering. Part of me obviously not thinking straight.

"I won't take no for an answer." She batted a pair of fake eyelashes that looked like spider webs shooting out of her forehead. Don't get those things, by the way.

"You will tonight." I turned away.

"Oh, that's it then, huh?" She called out after me. Not a fan of rejection, apparently. "What, too busy?"

My jaw clenched as I steeled myself for what was about to come.

"Too busy running your dad's business into the ground?"

A shot of rage lit me so fast that I almost laughed.

Almost.

I spun around and was an inch from her face faster than I could talk myself out of it. That drunk fight from her eyes evaporated. I didn't care that she started backing up, her hand searching for the table behind her. She'd pushed my buttons.

Correction—button.

Before I could unleash the stress I'd had pent up inside me, Jagg was between us in an instant, giving Leslie just enough balls to continue the assault.

"It's your way or the highway, Gunner. Always has been. People fall in line or they don't."

I pushed Jagg aside, my eyes pinning hers.

"Kind of like how your face fell in line with my zipper a few months ago?"

A gasp choked her throat. "You're an asshole, you know that, Steele?"

"I'm well aware, Miss Ambrose. Now, if you don't have someone escort you home, I will." My gaze dropped to her mouth. "And we all know how that's going to turn out."

Her eyes rounded in shock.

"Hey, now. Okay, alright, everyone relax..." Dallas jogged up, keys in hand. "Miss Leslie, let's get you on home now."

If fire could shoot out of eyes, Leslie's were like two torches.

She wasn't done.

"You need to take a load off, Gunner," She said while Dallas dragged her away. "No woman likes a man with baggage."

I turned and walked to my Harley, ignoring the hushed crowd watching my every move.

Baggage.

There was no doubt my baggage could do circles around hers but one thing was for sure—I wasn't going to find out. The last thing I needed in my life was a woman with more baggage than me.

4

LEXI

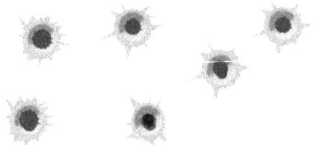

Somewhere between the bathroom and the hallway I'd found a sleek modern bar worthy of a James Bond movie. Beautiful women in glittering dresses, men in designer suits and ties. Each drinking martinis or bubbly glasses of champagne.

It was like a siren calling, hypnotizing me to enter into its realm.

Or, perhaps more fittingly, its anarchy, as I'd later find out.

I checked my reflection in the ornate gold mirror that hung outside the bar. That night, at Kara's urging, I'd dressed up. A pink silk tank tucked into a blue pinstripe skirt that did more than accentuate the curves that no amount of kickboxing classes could tame. The look was topped off with a pair of black six-inch heels and a killer knock-off Chanel clutch. I'd pulled my dark brown hair into a loose bun, for no other reason than I didn't have the energy to fight the frizz another day. All in all, an acceptable outfit for the establishment I was about to step into.

After a quick freshen up, I'd breezed into the bar like I

owned the place, and after the three shots I'd had, I probably thought I did.

"Champagne?" The tuxedo-clad bartender asked as if it wasn't a question.

"Please."

The twinkle in his eye as he delivered my bubbling flute told me the extra gloss was a good idea. The new pushup bra probably didn't hurt much either. Miracles those things can do, and I needed every bit of pushing I could get.

I stared down at my champagne, my stomach doing that little dip it had been doing since hearing the words, "You're fired."

What a week.

What a few months.

What a freaking decade.

I couldn't believe I'd failed my boss. My job. Worse than that, though, I'd failed myself. I was going to have to face the music the moment I got back to the states. A task that felt as challenging as undergoing another waterboarding.

I hadn't realized I'd downed my entire glass until I heard—

"Another champagne?" The barman walked up, his gaze lingering on my tank top.

"Better not, I've got to get back to—"

"A bottle of Dom, please." A deep, smooth voice sounded behind me as a shadow slid over the bar.

My stomach plummeted to my feet.

It took every bit of restraint I had to hide my shock as I turned into the bloated stomach of Sergei Orlov, aka, Bear. The Russian spy on the run. The reason I'd been fired.

I willed my pulse to slow and did my best southern gasp, accompanied with a hand over my heart, slipping seamlessly into my cover. "Well, Bear... I didn't expect to see you here."

He stared down at me a moment, a twinkle in those dark eyes, a tug at the corner of thin lips, parched from one too many kielbasas. Even through the dim lighting, I noticed a paleness in his skin that I hadn't seen before. A few more grey hairs that hadn't been there earlier.

The man was stressed.

And my internal red-flags were going off like crazy.

"May I sit?" He asked as he slid into the stool next to me, a faint scent of cigar smoke following seconds later.

The barman returned with two long stemmed glasses and a chilled bottle of hundred-dollar champagne. The cork popped, I giggled.

"Would you like me to pour your glasses, sir?"

Bear waved away the barman and reached for my glass, his eyes never leaving my face.

I went in. "I haven't seen you around the office lately..."

"I've been busy. So," he said, deflecting. "What brings you to this part of the world, Ms. Seaman?"

Seaman. The bastards who'd drawn up my fake identity no doubt had a laugh about that one. Joke on the "new trainee." I get it. But God knew I wouldn't forget it, for those asswipes had a grandé cup of ex-lax coming, complete with lithium-laced whip cream and caffeine-coated sprinkles.

I sipped the champagne and lifted the glass. "Girls trip, or, move-on-from-the-divorce trip. Either way, Cheers."

Our glasses clinked, he sipped. "You're alone?"

"My friends called it a night."

"No man to help get that divorce off your mind?"

"Not yet."

"I believe there are plenty men in here who would like to

give that a shot. Several who haven't stopped staring at you since you walked into the room."

I tipped my head, looking him over. "Well, who can compete with the bottle you just brought over, Mr. Orlov?"

"Bear."

"Bear."

"And..." he leaned in, the spice of his aftershave tickling my nose. "Not many men can."

I grinned although my gut was clenching. "That's quite the statement, Bear."

"Quite the heels, Ms. Seaman." His gaze dropped to my cleavage, then lifted back up to my lips, leaving a slithering feeling along my skin like a snail. Thank God for loofahs that could scrape off the first layer of your skin.

"Thank you. They're new. Got them half-price."

"You deserve more than a half-priced piece of pleather, Ms. Seaman."

I batted my lashes. "Do I?"

He smiled, then chugged the rest of his champagne. "Are you hungry?" He set down the empty flute.

My mind raced, the angel-devil thing on my shoulder. Pass? Or potentially... *get my job back.*

"I could eat," I said before I could talk myself out of it.

He grinned, then stood. "Shall we, then?"

I looped my arm through his, taking note of the two burly men who fell into step behind us. There were four men total with Bear, two bodyguards I'd guessed to be close to two-thirty each, both with matching Colt 1911s attached to their belts. Flashy, efficient, rich, deadly. That was their intended message. The one that I got, though, was former nerd-in-high school turned bouncer, turned ass-kissing security detail hypnotized by glitz, glamour, and rented double-D's every night. Because who wouldn't want to be close to the multi-millionaire who was suspected of running one of the biggest foreign espionage circles known to man?

I was led down a dark corridor with gold sconces on the walls, through a black door, then down another hallway and finally, through another door. This one red.

"Bear, lovely to see you this evening."

A woman of plastic perfection stood from behind a marble desk covered in flickering candles. It was an exclusive club if I'd ever seen one. I hadn't, by the way.

Her gaze flickered to me. "Table for two?"

"Private room."

"Of course." The mannequin gathered a few leather binders, then guided us behind a waterfalled wall. The room opened up to a sleek, spacious bar with glossy black walls and crystal chandeliers hanging above a trio of buck-naked strippers swaying to the low beat of jazz music. One blonde, one brunette, one black hair. Each more beautiful than the hostess.

A high-dollar strip club.

Holy crap, was all I could think.

Do they even have food at titty bars?

I'd heard Aruba was very "relaxed" on things like drugs and prostitution, but this was on a whole other level.

My eyes drifted from the naked bodies on stage to a dark corner where a man in a three-piece suit rested against the wall while a woman dined on his erection. A few booths down, two men, cocks in hands, watching two women dine on themselves.

The night was taking a turn.

"I hope this isn't too eccentric for you, Ms. Seaman."

"A bit."

He laughed, a condescending chuckle.

Asshole.

I was guided down a long hallway to the last room on the left. After unlocking several locks, the hostess pushed open the door.

"I'll have a bottle of Dom sent over right away and the waitress will take your orders."

"Thank you, Kiki."

Kiki. Because of course it was Kiki.

After receiving a hundo, the hostess smiled and left me to my newly-found redemption. Or death, I wasn't quite sure which would come first.

The room was small but breathtaking. Floor-to-ceiling windows overlooking the ocean. Stars twinkling in the sky. In the center, a round table with expensive china over white linen. To the side, a long couch over a shag carpet with more DNA on it than a used condom, I'd bet.

But it was the thin door in the corner that I kept my eye on.

"Impressed?" He asked.

I smiled my best naive southern divorcee smile. "I'd be lying if I said I wasn't."

"Sit."

I sat daintily on the edge of the couch as he handed me the menu.

"May I recommend the lobster or the filet? They're the best." He sat next to me.

I pretended to peruse the menu. My mind raced, my eyes kept flickering to that damn door.

"Let's see... I'll take the filet." I smiled and shrugged. "Can't take the south out of the girl, I guess."

He laughed and set the menu aside.

I put my hands on my knees.

"Don't be nervous," he said as he leaned in and swept a lock of hair behind my ear. My skin writhed under his touch. Pure disgust. Although I kept my head up, there was no mistaking the bulge in the guy's pants, or his other hand tracing it.

Nasty, nasty, Russian bastard.

I looked away.

"No?" He asked quietly.

I shook my head.

"Not now, then." He said with a chuckle as he relaxed against the couch, his gaze burning a hole in my back. "You know, Ms. Seaman, a woman of your stature deserves to have a little fun. Deserves fine things. Vacation homes in Italy, diamonds in each ear, all the Dom you can drink."

"I'm just an office assistant."

"Are you? Because I see much more." He leaned forward, resting his elbows on his knees and looked shamelessly at my breasts. "I see a woman who worked her way up from nothing, who values a good bottle of wine as much as that knockoff Chanel you're carrying. A woman who knows exactly her way around a fancy bar."

The second our eyes met, that little warning bell exploded. That little red flag that I'd been trained not to ignore.

My grip tightened around my glass.

"You sure think you know a lot about me, don't you?"

"I know you must be very good at your job."

He ran a finger down my arm, inciting a rush of goosebumps in sync with my increased pulse. The music had switched to a low, haunting melody as if a perfectly selected soundtrack to the moment slowly unfolding around me.

A moment that would forever change my life.

"It's a shame, though..." He continued...

My senses piqued, that shift from relaxed alert to imminent threat. The side door slowly opened and the same two bodyguards that had followed us earlier stepped out.

Tricky bastards.

One was all belly and muscle, a gluttonous combination. The other, fifty pounds less than Sausage Gut with a shifty look I'd seen before. A look that never ended well.

Bear nodded to the men, as I did, in an attempt to act like I wasn't thrown off.

"What's a shame?" I turned my attention back to Bear and smiled, my eyes sliding from the Beretta hidden behind his suit jacket to the windows overlooking the water.

I felt the air move behind me. I didn't move, I didn't blink. I stared back at Bear as my pulse roared in my ears.

"What's a shame, Bear?" I asked again, my voice a little stronger than intended.

"It's a shame that your company didn't provide you with a better cover, Miss York."

York.

I lunged off the couch a split-second before a fist grabbed my hair and yanked me back, sending my feet—and one heel—flying out from under me. My foot connected with the dining table, sending glasses, plates and candles clamoring to the floor. The shag rug lit like a Christmas tree, answering my question if lube was flammable. I rolled under the table and scrambled out the door as a bullet split the frame less than an inch from my ear.

And then, on cue, the screams rang out. Naked strippers, half-erect dongs flapping through the air as everyone took cover.

Another shot, this one whizzing past my forehead as I sprinted down the hallway to the bar.

"Get the car..." I remember hearing as I dove behind the barstools, pressing my body against the bar back. More

yells, screams—something in Russian—after another blast vibrated through the room. I squeezed myself down the bar, pulling my body down one stool to the next. A broken beer bottle sliced my thigh. Not that I cared, or even noticed. What I cared about was that I was nearing the end of the bar—the only cover I had.

My heart hammered as I raced to piece together a plan.

I zeroed in on the blinking exit sign behind a row of booths. Question was, how the heck was I going to get there? A bullet shattered the wood above my shoulder, another above my head. No time to think. I gripped the edge of the bar. Under a rain of bullets, I sprinted to the exit sign.

Pop, pop, pop, glasses, shards of wood, pictures shattered around me. I dove behind the booths but didn't stop, crawling across the floor like a baby chasing a pacifier. A very fast baby. I lunged under the exit sign, more bullets, more shouting.

"Poluchit yeye! Puluchit yeye!" I knew that one. 'Get her,' in Russian.

I sprinted down another hall and flung myself out the back door. The briny smell of ocean whipped past me in a humid gust. I frantically swiped the hair from my eyes as Bear's bodyguards emerged from the corner. The other two men he'd been with earlier had been lost in the scuffle somewhere inside... I hoped so, anyway.

One thing was for sure—Bear didn't travel alone. I kicked off my one remaining heel and took off down a dark alley between zipping bullets and pounding footsteps. The reflection of headlights bounced off the buildings around me and based on the low growl of the engine, I deciphered it was Bear's coveted 200K Maybach, coming for me from behind.

I rounded a corner and stopped cold. I was trapped. In

front of me stood a ten foot fence, secured between two soaring buildings with a chain and lock. Beyond that, a dark parking lot. Beyond that, the glittering lights of nightlife.

Like a rat in a maze, I was trapped.

Heavy footsteps descended, car doors slamming in the distance.

Like a beacon through the night, the headlights sparked off a narrow metal door in one of the buildings. Unlocked. Hope sparked as I swung open the door and hurled myself up the steps.

A parking garage. Perfect.

I raced up at least eight flights of stairs, heavy footsteps below me. Gasping for breath, I reached the top floor and burst through the metal door. I'd expected a lot full of fancy cars, what I got was a bare rooftop with ventilation pipes and a few blinking lights.

... And absolutely nowhere to run.

The door behind me flew open followed by a pistol rushing my face.

Shit.

Chest heaving, I raised my hands and backed up, scanning the scene around me. Nothing but endless black ocean in the distance, a busy street below and a long way to fall. I focused again on the gun in Sausage Gut's hand, then the lack of one in Shifty's. Probably on the barroom floor somewhere. I had a feeling that didn't matter. I had a feeling Shifty was just as lethal without his pistol.

Two against one.

My heels hit the edge of the building.

Red blinking lights silhouetted my Russian attackers from behind as they stepped toward me.

Kill or capture, I wondered? Kill me because I knew too much, or capture me and torture for everything I knew?

My question was answered when Sausage Gut narrowed his sights.

Kill.

I lurched to the side as the blast echoed through the air. Two bodies lunged toward me, with Sausage leading the pack. With my back to the ledge, it was either fight or die. I grit my teeth and charged Sausage, throwing myself onto him like a spider monkey. The air expelled from my lungs with his weight as we rolled across the roof floor. My knee connected with his groin, my hand scrambling for the gun in his hand. A well timed elbow jab loosened his hold, giving me just enough time to grab the gun from his hand and put a bullet between his eyes.

I jumped up, pointed the gun at Shifty, who lunged forward and after a quick shuffle, knocked it from my hands.

Yeah, he was the fighter of the crew.

A right hook was answered back with a hook of his own. I felt the *pop* a split second before the blood poured out, the metallic taste sending a firestorm of adrenaline through my veins. I swiped left, then right. He caught my wrist, twisted and turned. My body followed the flow, my back turning against him.

Not good.

"You put up one hell of a fight, bitch."

"You have no idea." I sent the back of my head into his nose. Based on the warm spray on the back of my neck, I guessed I'd broken it.

He shoved me forward, the momentum too great to stop. I watched the narrow edge coming at me with each inch I flew through the air. A dark abyss ending on the concrete sidewalk. Of all the things I thought would kill me, falling off a parking garage was not one of them. I threw my weight to the ground, my body slamming against the edge.

One more inch. One more inch and I would have been roadkill.

Shifty appeared over me with a bloody, crooked grin on his face. My attempt to push up and fight was met with a boot in my face. I'd seen stars before but nothing like that. To be honest, I think I passed out for a second before the world started spinning around me. I was confused and disoriented—the last thing you'd want while up against a ledge with a hundred foot drop.

I felt Shifty grab my hair then my shoulders. One heave later, my head was dangling over the ledge.

I remember it so vividly—the breeze through my hair, the rush of blood to my brain. Then, with the next push, my shoulders met the wind. It was that moment, that weightless moment that shook me from my daze and sent an ice-cold panic though my veins. The will to survive. I was suddenly awake, alert and very aware that I was about to take my last breath before my body obliterated the sidewalk below.

Hands gripped my waist...

With a guttural scream, I slammed my foot between his legs and propelled Shifty over me. I remember hearing the whoosh of his body as it fell through the air. The distant *splat* as I scrambled back onto the roof.

And then the screams.

Gasping for air, I took a frantic look around the roof to make sure none of Bear's other cronies had joined the party. Then, I dropped my head between my knees for one, two, three breaths.

Finally, I swiped the blood from my nose and pushed to a stance. My gaze drifted to the dead man a few feet away.

The man I'd just killed.

One of two.

A cloud drifted from the moon, a silver beam running along black ocean below.

My gut twisted.

I'd been outed, exposed, my cover blown. Bear and his endless network of stone-cold killers knew my real name.

And I thought I was at rock bottom twenty-four hours ago.

I listened to the chaos emanating below—and one thing became crystal clear.

I needed to hide.

Quick.

5

LEXI

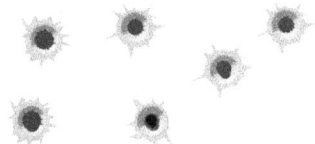

The escape...

The bass of the bar above me shook the dingy, cracked mirror as I stared at my reflection. I gripped the sink in a feeble attempt to steady the tremors vibrating through my body. Claw marks, that I didn't even remember getting, ran down my neck, my knuckles and elbows were scraped raw. My hair was a matted mess of dirt and clotted blood. Spatters of blood dotted my pink tank top, in an ironic twist, looking more like a trendy abstract design than a struggle for my life.

A life that was still at risk unless I got off that island. An *island,* of all freaking places, to be exposed as an undercover agent.

Luck was not on my side.

Bear and his bodyguards had my purse, wallet, my room key, my Dallas apartment keys, my life. Worse than all that was the fact that they had my cell phone—access to all my emails, both personal and professional, including confidential information indicating that Astor Stone and the US government were investigating him on the assumption that he was a Russian spy. I assumed Bear would have no trouble breaking my phone password because I doubted a pesky thing like security would be a challenge for a Russian spy. I did have one little thing, though. My passport that I'd slipped into my pocket after showing it to the waitress. That was it. They had everything else.

International incident?

No doubt about it.

The headline would read: *International incident triggered by careless, undercover spy wanna-be loser.*

No... more like: *Funeral arrangements are under way for careless, undercover spy wanna-be loser who incited an international incident.*

Astor's words echoed in my ear like a punch in the gut.

"I want to make it clear, Miss York, if your cover is blown, Astor Stone will deny having any knowledge of your visit to Texas. There will be no cavalry coming over the hill for you."

I was totally completely, utterly alone. In another country. On an island.

My stomach rolled and before I could catch myself, I bent over and vomited into the brown-rimmed sink.

For the second time.

Shit, shit, shit, shit. I was losing it. I needed to pull myself together.

I needed to act. Quick.

After splashing cold water on my face and brushing my teeth with my finger, I wrapped my long, brown hair into a bun and slid it under the *Granny's Stop 'n Go* hat I'd swiped while sneaking to the gas station bathroom. I'd untucked my tank, yanking it over the skirt as much as I could. After slipping into the flip flops I'd stolen from a trio of passed-out hippies on the sidewalk, I counted the cash I'd also pulled from their pockets. Thirty-six dollars, a bottle of pills and one doobie, which was as good as cash in Aruba. I took a deep breath and made my way out of the bathroom.

My eyes darted around the store. An elderly man sat alone in a plastic booth nursing a cup of coffee. A pair of prostitutes giggling next to the condoms, which, by the way, was the largest selection of birth control I'd ever seen. The clerk, a sixty-something woman with flaming red hair mindlessly popped her gum behind the counter. The low chatter of a local news station drifted through the air. Outside, drones of people going to and from the bars. Enjoying life while I was trying to save mine.

I darted from one aisle to the next, keeping my eye on that front door. There was no question Bear and his Russians would come after me. I knew too much and I'd seen too much, including all of their faces. They probably thought I'd been wired and had recorded the entire incident.

I was as good as *dead*.

My stomach rolled again. Everything was beginning to take its toll. The liquor I'd had at the bar with Bev and Kara, the adrenaline from surviving a physical fight, the shock of killing two men, and finally, the fear. The doubt. All confidence I had was gone.

I was scared—petrified.

Pulling my cap down low, I squared my shoulders and stepped outside into the humid night air, the thumping of EDM matching my pounding heart. A crowd of mini-skirts and six-inch heels sauntered by giving me just enough cover until I saw my salvation, a bright yellow taxi barreling down the road.

Twenty minutes and all my cash later, I was at the Aruba airport standing in line with my plane ticket I'd printed from an Internet cafe along the way, where I'd also sent Kara and Bev an email telling them I'd decided to head back early. I'd given the ticket agent some song and dance about needing to fly out early because of a family emergency. Between that and the little blue pills, she was more than happy to add me to the standby list.

Six hours later, I landed at the Dallas International Airport, with no cash, no credit cards, no car. I took off on foot in the forty-something degree weather in only a tank top, ripped skirt, baseball cap, and flip flops. Hours and hours I walked through the dark night, a freezing mist the icing on the cake. Hours of replaying what had happened. Hours of wondering what the future held for me.

Miles I walked, miles of fighting tears that came with fatigue and hunger mixing in my system like a toxic poison.

Then, the universe decided to shoot me a solid. Sometime in the wee hours of the morning, a man in a rusted Chevy with silver hair and kind, blue eyes pulled over and offered me a ride. I offered him the gold earrings my mother had gotten me on my sixteenth birthday for his tin can on wheels.

Five minutes later I bid farewell to my new guardian angel, leaving him at a trucker's cafe waiting on his wife to pick him up, and me driving into the black night.

Heading to the only place I could think of.

The one place I didn't want to go.

6

GUNNER

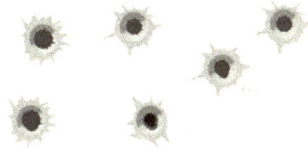

Forty one, forty two, forty three.
Forty four.

I stared down at the bone-colored tiles with little blue specks. Head bowed, my forearms rested on my knees, my ass on the boulder they called a couch.

Four hundred and forty-four twelve-inch tiles in the room.

One hundred and six times I'd counted each one since my brother had caught a bullet to the brain and been admitted to ICU.

I blew out a breath, my eyes mindlessly drifting from each blue speck on the tile below my boots.

The face of a wolf.

A hooded grim reaper.

A jack-o-lantern.

A pair of oblong breasts.

A gangly-looking penis.

I'd created every picture known to man from those little specks in tile number four hundred forty-four.

Unlike my brothers who sat and stared at Feen during

their shifts, I couldn't even look at the guy. My skin crawled like ants just being in the same room.

Sounds fucked up, I know, but hear me out.

You see, growing up, Feen was always the leader. *Always.* Except his relationship with the twins, Gage and Ax, was different than his and mine. With our younger brothers, Feen was more of a father than a brother, mainly due to the fact that our dad was never home. Being the director of the NSA tended to eat up all your free time.

Feen taught the twins how to swim, he taught them right from wrong, how to take care of themselves, take care of our land, how to fight. I'd watched both Gage and Ax become dependent on his guidance. On his approval. They put him on a pedestal. Rightly so. The guy spent every second worrying about his little brothers and taking care of them.

Yes, Phoenix was, by all counts, the leader of the household.

The star Steele brother.

I was born thirteen months after Phoenix. From the day I came out of the womb, I was at odds with the guy—according to dad, anyway. We fought like cats and dogs about everything, from toys, to clothes, to food, to women. Anything and everything, Feen and I disagreed about it.

It wasn't until the day of my seventeenth birthday that things really came to a head. I'd spent the morning polishing up my pride and joy, a 1971 Chevy Cheyenne, baby blue. She was my first vintage restoration and the beginning of a life-long obsession that had me spending more time in the garage than in my own bed. Then, after a new tattoo—another soon-to-be-obsession—me and a few of my buddies had taken to the woods with a case of PBR, a handle of Jack, a bag of beef jerky, and a pack of freshman girls. Hours went on, the bonfire raged, cans and bottles were emptied. People I didn't know had shown up.

It was a small-town Saturday night party. On steroids.

Night drifted to early morning... And that's when I heard a scream.

In a daze of whiskey and confusion, I followed the whimpers where I found a drunk redneck with his hands on a teenage girl's chest.

Three seconds later, the guy was on his back with a black eye and broken hand.

Three more seconds after that, all hell broke loose. A good ol' southern brawl—until Phoenix rode up on his white horse with sword waving. Or, was it white knight? Something like that. I watched the guy singlehandedly dismantle the brawl, including bloodying a few of my buddies' lips. That wasn't cool. So I did the only thing my whiskey induced stubborn ass knew to do. I confronted the raging bull and told him to leave. I didn't need him handling my shit like he did with the twins.

I still don't know who took the first punch but that day, Phoenix broke my nose and fractured my cheek bone. Unintentional—whatever—but damage that included a few stitches was done. Shortly after the bloodshed, the cops broke up the event. Feen, the only eighteen year old at the party, was arrested for aiding and abetting a minor. I'd told him he deserved it, and he told me I deserved what I got. The difference was, he was right and I was wrong. Feen didn't deserve to go to jail that night, and I absolutely deserved a shattered nose for challenging my brother, my own flesh and bone. Especially in front of other people. After that incident, our relationship was never the same. Don't get me wrong, we'd take a bullet for each other, but that brotherly camaraderie was gone.

Disintegrated.

Funny thing was, I don't think anyone really noticed. I'd told dad and the twins that someone else had kicked my ass. He didn't care. Dad only cared that I'd been the reason that his precious Phoenix had gone to jail.

Because, I, Gunner Steele, was always the troublemaker of the family. The bad egg. The screw up. The letdown. Gage was... well, whatever the heck Gage was. Ax was the golden boy. Straight A's his whole freaking life. Who does that? And Phoenix was the leader of us all, the heir to Duke Steele's throne.

I was thirteen the first time I was arrested. Public intox. Still blamed Jagg's grandma for that one. Who the hell drinks spiked lemonade at ten in the morning? My next arrest came a year later for fighting... then a few more for fighting, then one for indecent exposure—I'm taking that one to the grave—then later, a DWI that landed me a few nights in the county jail.

After that—and an unfortunate experience with a sexually confused inmate that ended with me in solitary confinement—I'd told myself I was going to change. I followed in my brother's and dad's footsteps, enlisted in the Marines, and to my shock as much as everyone else's, I excelled. Over the years, I became one of the top snipers in the country.

I'd finally found a purpose, something that I was good at. A way to funnel all my teenage rage and regret into something that meant something. I was a damn good soldier. We all were. My brothers and I were living the life we were meant to live. A life that we loved.

Until a bastard named the Knight Fox murdered my dad and put a bullet in Feen's skull, sending my entire family on its head. After that, my brothers and I went on the hunt, twenty-four-seven—when we weren't sitting in Phoenix's hospital room, anyway. Each of us took rotating, four hour shifts to ensure one of us would be there if something happened. If our older brother died.

That was my sixth four-hour shift and I still couldn't look at Feen for more than two seconds.

Why?

Because I couldn't stand to see the true leader—the *real* leader—of our family suffering.

Because Phoenix Steele didn't deserve what happened to him.

I did.

It fucking should have been me. I should be the one lying in the hospital bed. It should have been me. That very thought had stolen every second of sleep from me since the incident. I was a shell of a man. Empty, except for the unrelenting rage funneling through my veins like speed.

So, I counted. During my shifts, I counted tiles. Just like I was doing when a rapid succession of beeps tore my focus away and had me surging to my feet.

One of the machines coming out of Feen's body lit up like a Christmas tree.

I leapt to the foot of my brother's bed.

The door opened and a nurse hurried in. My heart hammered as I watched her check the machine, check the tubes, check him.

"Sorry about that." The machine finally went silent. "Everything's okay."

I exhaled the breath I didn't realize I'd been holding and stared at my brother, the wires coming out of his chest, the IV's in both his arms. They'd pulled him from his medically induced coma, which was a good sign, but his skin had turned a waxier shade of grey the last few days. His weight was dropping quickly. I don't know which he'd hate worse.

It was an image I would never get out of my head.

The nurse continued, "His body is adjusting to being out of the coma and off the breathing and feeding tube. The next few days are critical."

"How's his breathing?"

"Erratic. More shallow than it has been. We're monitoring it closely."

"Is he..." I shocked myself by not being able to finishing the sentence.

"Getting worse?"

"Yeah." I shoved my hands into my pockets.

She paused long enough to make my stomach sink.

"We're keeping an extra close eye on him."

I cleared my throat and forced myself to look at him again. "No new brain scans, right?"

"Doc's got one scheduled for tomorrow, I believe. As discussed, he has damage to his right frontal lobe, the consequences of which are yet to be determined."

"Meaning, you still don't even know if he'll be able to walk, talk, eat, or take care of himself when he wakes."

"If he wakes, and yes, that's right. There're too many variables right now, but I will say, your brother is one of the toughest humans I've had the pleasure of meeting."

I swallowed the knot in my throat as a moment of silence slid between us.

"Well, Mr. Steele, I'll leave you alone."

I nodded as she stepped out.

Mr. Steele.

Mr. Steele.

I sank back down onto the couch.

Not a single person had ever called me Mr. Steele until after Feen's incident.

I hated it.

I scrubbed my hands over my face, grinding my teeth to stifle the scream wanting to bust out of me. My pulse roared in my ears, rage threatening to boil over.

It should have been me.

It should have been me.

It fucking should have been me.

I surged to Feen's bedside, unable to contain the tornado of emotions swirling inside me. It was the closest I'd been to him since the incident.

"Phoenix. Brother." The words came out in a whispered growl as I hovered beside him. "Brother. My brother." I repeated. "I'm sorry. I'm sorry for not living up to what you wanted me to be. What I needed to be. I'm sorry for being a little pissant. I'm sorry for letting you down, for letting Dad down." My lips curled to a snarl to counteract the quiver. "Hear me, brother, I will *not* let you down again. I will hunt the Knight Fox until his last breath." Uncontrollable tears burned my eyes. "I will find him, Phoenix, and I will kill him." My hand found his under the blanket. "And you will watch me kill him. Because you're going to pull through. You're going to be okay. You've. *Got. This.* I love you brother. We'll see each other again soon."

Chatter outside the hospital door had me snapping out of the crazed emotions taking over my body.

I pulled my hand away, sniffed the snot away and glanced at the clock—2:24am.

Two more hours until my shift was up.

After splashing cold water on my face, I resumed my normal position on the couch over tile number four-hundred and forty four, head bowed, elbows on knees.

And I let the fucking tears fall.

. . .

5:04am

The icy air whipped around my leather jacket as I barreled up the long, windy driveway. The night was as black as coal and cold as shit. If Stan the weatherman was correct, we were in for our first freeze of the season tomorrow night.

Dead leaves spun around me as I reached the top of the mountain and burst onto the circle drive of the main house where my brothers, Dallas, myself, and several staff lived. It was an eight-thousand square foot monstrosity of solid rock and wood. Every upscale amenity you could find, including a theater, elevator, indoor and outdoor pool, basketball courts, you name it. A cozy log cabin on steroids. Okay, cocaine maybe. Honestly, I'd just as soon have a one-bedroom next to the shooting range. Add ESPN and a keg and I might not ever leave the place.

I pulled into our ten-car garage and cut the engine.

"Mornin'." Wolf, former Marine turned head of security for Steele Shadows, peeked up from behind a brand-spanking-new Harley Davidson Fat Boy complete with satin chrome finishes and a 114 big twin engine with enough power to give a monk a boner.

"Holy hell, man." I slid off my own and crossed the garage.

"She's a beauté, ain't she?"

I ran my finger over the shiny black fender. "Damn. When'd you get her?"

"Last week. She's been in and out of the shop getting customized. Gotta keep up with you."

He nodded to Shayna, the gleaming apple-red 1966 Ford Mustang I'd fully restored with my bare hands. Wasn't quite road ready but getting there. His brow cocked. "Trade ya."

"Not on your life, pal. What's got you shining the bike up at five thirty in the morning?"

I didn't ask why he was awake. Like my brothers and I, we never slept. Blame it on our old day jobs. Even though Wolf had a cabin a few miles off the property, the guy spent nearly every minute at the main house. Had his own little crash pad, and now, a section of our garage, apparently.

"We got a new client."

"What? Here? Now?... When?"

"The alert that someone passed onto the property went off at three-fifty a.m., to be exact. Beat up Chevy with more rust on it than that vintage dodge you've got sitting outside the shooting range."

"Leave Cheryl out of this."

He snorted. "Anyway, you know, Celeste would usually handle the meet and greet and booking in, but..." his face dropped. "You know."

"Wait, so they're still here? You already booked them in as a client? Dude, you can't just—"

His eyes met mine with a look that had my back straightening. The only way Wolf would book a client without consulting with us is if he truly believed they were in imminent danger.

And *dammit*, the last thing in the world I wanted to deal with was someone who was in imminent danger.

"An exposed UC."

"An exposed undercover agent?"

"Yep."

"No shit? Which agency?"

"Astor Stone."

"Christ." I ran my fingers through my hair. Not many people knew what Astor Stone really did. Only top level executives and a few elite military teams. My brothers and I

knew them well. They were notorious for claiming ignorance and feeding exposed agents to the wolves to cover their own asses.

"What's the story?"

"Not sure. Was pretty tight-lipped."

"Tight-lipped? No. We need to understand everything—every *single* thing—in order to provide the best protection."

"It was four in the damn morning, Gunner. Wait till the sun rises."

"I can't believe you didn't—" I stopped. Arguing with Wolf was pointless and I was running on empty. "Who gets him? Gage? He's run security detail for a few CIA agents before."

"Nope. Gage got a new client yesterday."

"Ax?"

"Nope. Same."

"Dammit," I spat out.

Something twinkled in Wolf's dark eyes. "Don't be so quick to judge there, Judy."

"Why not?"

"It's a *she*. Not a *he*."

My brows popped up. "A *she* Astor Stone agent?"

He clicked his tongue and shook his head. "Now, Celeste really wouldn't approve of the sexist undertones of that comment, Gunn."

No she wouldn't. Celeste would have my neck in a lock.

"What's her name?"

He shrugged.

"You book a client without knowing her name?"

"Do I need to remind you again that it was four in the morning? And she was super jumpy, hyper. I didn't push cause we all know I'm not the best with jumpy women."

Damn, I missed Celeste.

"I booked her in telling her that someone would be with her first thing in the morning."

"Thank God you don't run your own company, Wolf."

"I know, right? Anyway, she showed up with nothing. I think Dallas packed a bag of clothes, you know, women shit. She had me take it down to the cabin. I set it on the porch."

"Nice effort. How did you know what size she wore?"

"I didn't, Dallas did. Checked her image on the security cams and did her best guess. Celeste has an entire closet of clothes for clients, you know."

Did I know that? No, I didn't because Celeste always handled that kind of stuff. Especially with female clients.

I rubbed my temples, willing away the impending headache.

"There's one more thing—" Wolf stood.

"You haven't given me one thing at all."

"She specifically asked *not* for you."

I blinked. "What?"

"She straight up told me she wanted anyone to take her case *but you.*"

A second ticked by.

"Are you serious?"

"Yep. As serious as she was, and let me tell you, she was pretty damn serious."

"Do I know her?"

"How the hell should I know?"

"Is she from around here?"

A shrug.

"God*dammit,* Wolf."

He grinned.

"So, this chick rolls up at four in the morning, tells you she's an outed UC with an investigation company secretly contracted with the US government, and tells you she's in trouble but wants anyone *but me* to be her assigned bodyguard."

"Pretty much."

I threw my hands up in a childish display that I wasn't proud of. "Give her to Gage. Give her to Ax. Fuck, *you* take her."

"No, no, and *hell* no."

I blew out a breath. "Fine... *fine*. Where is this mystery woman?"

"Cabin 3."

7

GUNNER

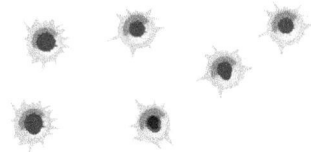

My grip tightened around the steering wheel of the ATV as I drove down the pebbled path through the woods.

An outed undercover agent who wanted nothing to do with me.

I'd run through every woman I knew who worked at Astor Stone in my head, which was zero. Then, I considered every woman I'd pissed off at some point, which was countless. Then, I considered every woman I'd slept with and not called back. That list spanned several decades and several continents.

Dammit.

For all I knew, this mystery client could be best friends with the she-devil herself, Leslie Ambrose. That had to be it. Women always hated who their friend did, right?

I wasn't sure if it was the lack of sleep, food, booze, whatever, but I found myself thinking about how I interacted with women. Which, I can say with one-hundred percent confidence, was something I'd never thought about before. Cared about, even.

The entire world knew I was a man of few words. I knew I wasn't the smoothest talker. The thing was, I didn't *want* to be. I didn't have time to sugar-coat or kiss someone's ass. Hell, I'd rather have an enema filled with hydrochloric acid than kiss someone's ass. Having the patience to think about what I said before it came out of my mouth, or worse, censoring it, was inconceivable. It wasn't me. Take it or leave it.

And maybe that was the problem.

How was *someone like me* going to run a successful private security firm? *If* worst-case-scenario happened to Feen. Me, a CEO? Might as well have a hooker give the next sermon at your local seventh-day Adventist church. Didn't work.

Didn't fit.

And now, my take-it-or-leave-it attitude had bled over to a client not wanting to work with me.

Me—*I*—was officially affecting business. The business my dad had built from the ground up.

Not cool.

Not fucking cool at all and it had my jaw clenching and head spinning.

At what point could I just live my own damn life?

At what point would everyone be okay with that?

... What would it take for me to look in the mirror and change?

I knew when. Deep in my gut, I knew when.

The moment I put a bullet in the Knight Fox's head.

After that, I'd change. Until then, though, everyone could go screw themselves.

Feeling more irritated than rational now, I sped up the narrow driveway that led to Cabin 3.

To my surprise, the place was lit up. Considering it was

six in the morning and our mystery guest arrived at four, I assumed she would have been asleep.

Well, that was the first of many surprises to come.

I rolled to a stop next to the cabin and got out. The early morning was still as black as midnight and as cold as a penguin's pecker. The mist had dissipated but was replaced with a howling wind that reminded me of the dead of winter.

My breaths came out in puffs as I turned to head to the porch when movement in the window caught my eye. Behind sheets of sheer curtains—Up, down, up, down, up, down, a long, pony-tail bobbed up and down. I cocked my head. As any man with a beating heart would do, I stepped closer, a fully imagined single-girl porno already playing in my head.

Unfortunately, I didn't get knees in the air. What I got was a curvy silhouette sprinting like a cheetah on the treadmill. The long strides, the smooth movement of a seasoned runner. Not like those bouncy girls with matching spandex that don't break a sweat. No, this chick was hitting it. Hard. At six o'clock in the morning. And, by the way, the only thing I hated more than a sunrise workout was a morning person.

I watched her a moment longer than I cared to admit, then rounded the cabin and banged on the door.

Nothing.

I tried again, the force of each knock matching my already non-existent patience.

Still, nothing.

I'm not proud to admit that her lack of opening the door felt like rejection number two of the day. The first being her insistence that I have nothing to do with her. What did it say that she'd rather go without personal security than have me help her? Yep, six in the morning and already facing two rejections from a woman I didn't even know.

I stomped off the steps and went around to the back deck which was a bit closer to the bedroom. Banged on that door.

Nothing.

Muttering curses I'd only heard Dallas say when she'd smeared a manicure, I went back to the front and knocked again, this time, breaking skin on one of my knuckles. And that was the straw that broke the camel's back.

Grinding my teeth, I keyed in the universal security code that only me, my brothers, Wolf, and Celeste knew, and pushed through the door.

REEEEEEEEEEE... the sound of the winding treadmill belt buzzed through the air, along with the scent of something vanilla-y.

"Hello," I called out and slammed the door behind me.

No response.

"Hello! *Yo!*" I snapped as I stalked through the living room to the bedroom door.

Her scream rivaled any pre-teen at a shirtless Bieber concert. But that was nothing compared to the one that came out of her when her foot slipped off the treadmill. A flash of red, black, brown hair, and pale flesh propelled into the air, then slammed into the back wall, sending a single Nike flying into the ceiling fan.

"Oh, *shit.*" I darted into the bedroom, ripped the treadmill cord from the socket and spun around to the body crumpled between the wall and treadmill.

The chick shot up like a feral cat from behind a dumpster.

"What the *hell* are you doing?" She screamed from the other side of the treadmill.

As if independent of my body, my gaze shot down to a pair of perky, pillow-soft breasts still jiggling from momentum and curves that should have had their own caution sign.

Her body swayed back and forth. I recognized the stance. Elbows bent at her sides, fingers flexed, weight shifting to the balls of her feet. A spark in those dark, almond eyes, the color of aged whiskey.

The woman was ready to fight.

I'd be lying if I said I didn't consider having a throw down with her. Wearing only a red sports bra and black spandex shorts, I could see every arc, every angle, every erect nipple on her staggeringly-sexy body. Waves of sweat shimmered off of tanned skin as smooth as butter. The tone of her muscles told me she lived a disciplined life but the pin-up girl tattooed on her bicep told me she had just enough spunk to make things interesting in the bedroom. Then there was that face. Sharp lines matching the venom in her stance, a pair of lush, honeyed lips as plump as her breasts. Her eyes, a hint of gold against a deep brown, daring me with a confidence that told me she didn't take orders. From anyone.

Which was a shame, because the moment she'd stepped foot inside Cabin 3, she was mine. Mine to listen to, mine to mind. Mine to obey.

And she was about to find that out the hard way.

"I *said,* what the *hell* are you doing?" She repeated, her arms wrapping around her midsection.

Confusion had my head tilting.

Was she insecure?

Of *that* body?

I caught a better glance of that tattoo. A Rosie the Riveter depiction of a beautiful, voluptuous woman with a string of yarn wrapped around her arm, the ball sitting next to her high-heeled feet. Interesting, and yeah, sexy as *hell*.

I put one foot on the treadmill and extended my hand. "Here. Let me—"

She swatted my hand away. I didn't like that so I reached down and grabbed it myself. With a huff, she lifted her leg, then whimpered.

"You okay?"

"Yeah." She yanked her hand away and limped across the treadmill. I took a few steps back, my attention now focusing on her clenched fists more than her breasts.

She stared at me, chest heaving, nostrils flared, and slammed her hands on those deliciously curvy hips.

"I'm not going to ask you again. What are you *doing breaking into my cabin?!*" She squealed, sending the hair on the back of my neck standing.

*Geez*us.

I held up my hands, fighting the urge to plug my ears. The drums can only handle so much. *"Listen,* lady. I knocked, several times. Even went around to the back. You didn't answer. I let myself in."

She blinked a few times, then her eyes rounded before sliding over my body from head to toe. Usually, this kind of move was the prequel to a flirty banter that ended between two sheets. Instead, this woman's once-over ended in scowl of disgust.

"You're Gunner Steele, aren't you?" The disdain in her voice was evident, dissolving any attraction I might have had initially.

I dipped my chin. "I'd say pleasure to meet you but for some reason, I don't think that's the case."

She snorted, crossed her arms over her chest, then winced. I looked down at the strip of road rash—make that belt rash—running down her arm, shiny and oozing already. Above that, an elbow that was already two sizes too big.

"Come here." I said.

"No."

"Come here."

"I'm fine."

"Come *here*. You're hurt."

"I'm fine."

"*Christ* woman, if you really are in some sort of a problem, the last place you need to go is a hospital when that thing gets infected, where you'll have to answer all sorts of personal questions."

What felt like a full minute slid by before she conceded.

Damn this woman.

I turned and crossed the living room. "You coming? Or would you like to take another spin down the treadmill?"

I didn't hear her, instead, I felt her behind me as I stepped into the kitchen. Not her presence so much as the attitude weighing down the room by a few tons.

I set the first aid kit on the stove, gripped her waist and hoisted her onto the counter.

As expected, she did not like this.

And because of that, I did.

I also noticed she'd put on a long T-shirt over her clothes. I was both disappointed and confused that this woman wanted to conceal that banging body. *Women*. An enigma I'd never figure out. Didn't care to, to be totally honest.

"Put this ice on your elbow." I said. "I'll lay out a few heat packs for you. Alternate—"

"Every fifteen minutes, I know."

I shook my head, half of me wanting to take a quick peek in her shorts to make sure this woman didn't have a penis.

"You shouldn't run with headphones in." I ripped the top of an antiseptic wipe.

"You're joking. I was on a treadmill."

"Nope. Figured a UC would know that."

"Oh, you mean how running with headphones *outside* takes away one of your most precious sensors and decreases the chances of a woman being aware of an imminent threat? Like a lurking kidnapper, a rapist, or someone peeking in your windows, perhaps? *Or* how about the fact that sixty-eight percent of pedestrians killed while wearing headphones are men? And over sixty percent of those men are under thirty years old? No, I don't know a thing about headphones and personal safety. Enlighten me."

She didn't wait for me to respond. Nope, she continued with—

"And besides, this little piece of advice from a guy who breaks into a stranger's place in the middle of the night?"

"First, this is my cabin. I own it."

She looked away.

"Second, it's morning."

"It's dark. You could have gotten yourself killed."

I couldn't fight a grin at this, or the well-timed application of the antiseptic. She didn't flinch, though. One point for her.

"What's your name?"

"Lexi."

I felt her eyes boring into the side of my face.

"Got a last name, Lexi?"

"York," she said with a sort of punctuation in her voice as if I should know. No, I didn't know a Lexi York. Or, remember one, for that matter.

"Is that your real name, or your cover?"

"Real. My cover was Sherry Seaman."

My eyes lifted to hers. "What were you? A stripper?"

"In your dreams."

"No, Miss York, in my dreams the strippers can actually stay on moving objects."

The bobbing of her head told me I was getting the sarcastic nod of a twelve-year old girl.

I slapped on the bandage. "Gonna scab over. We'll take off the bandage tomorrow, let it breathe." I looked up into narrowed eyes that reminded me of Dallas when I used to steal candy bars from her secret stash when I was a kid.

I took a step back. "Now that you're all bandaged up, first thing's first, *ma'am*..."

Her eyebrows popped with my sarcasm.

"I'll need to do a thorough assessment of your case before signing you on—"

"*Before* signing me on?" She hopped off the counter. Damn those jiggling boobs. Hypnotic they were, and ironically so because they weren't that big. Just... perfect.

"But I thought—"

"And during that assessment you'll need to provide me with every piece of information you have, as well as details about what you're perceiving as a threat. Then, I'll let you know."

"You'll let me *know?*"

"That's right."

"Well, let *me* let *you* know this: Shepherd said—"

"Wolf."

"Wolf. Oh. Yeah. Anyway, *Wolf* made it sound like it was a done deal. I'm here, under Steele Shadows protection, and that one of your brothers will handle my case."

"Sorry, sweetheart. You're stuck with me." I turned and

breezed out of the kitchen. "Heating pads are in the second drawer to the left of sink. Instructions are on the back."

A pair of little pounding footsteps followed. "But—"

I stopped mid-stride and spun on my heel, where a pantsless simmering attitude barreled into my chest.

She stumbled backward.

"Listen, you don't like me, that much is obvious. I don't give a shit." I glowered down at her. "I don't care why, so keep it to yourself. You're here because you feel like you need protection. I'm it. Stay or leave."

She blinked, a slight stun on her face.

I turned around walked to the door. "I'll be back in an hour and we'll start from there."

I'd expected another protest, but made it out the front door with nothing but a slam.

A gust of cold air cooled my heated neck. Truth was, we could have had our meeting right then and there. But I needed a minute to calm down, regain my patience.

A minute to digest the fact that I'd just been handed another short-tempered, cagey client to babysit.

A client that couldn't stand to be in the same room as me.

I blew out a breath and stepped off the porch.

Another fucking day in paradise.

8

LEXI

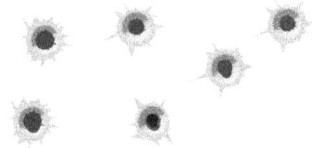

*J*erk.

Asshole.

Womanizer.

Sexy as *hell*.

I thought it was the man known as *'Good-for-nothing Gunner'* when he'd stepped into the bedroom and scared the living daylights out of me—a moment I still wasn't sure if I was more pissed or humiliated about. It wasn't until I saw the sleeves of tattoos that I knew it was him for sure. He was exactly as my sister had described. Tall, tanned, ruggedly handsome with shaggy brown hair and muscles that rippled like a washboard. The one thing she'd failed to mention was the one thing I noticed first—those eyes. A deep indigo, as dark as the ocean, the kind of color that made you want to take a second look. But it was the black rim around the irises that pulled me in. A dark gloom imprisoning the vibrant color, dulling it, encaging the beauty that was screaming to get out.

Disconcerting.

Alluring.

The former Marine was the biggest guy I'd ever seen, aside from the ones in those superhero movies, with an aloof, yet commanding presence that told me he would neither coddle me, nor put up with any bull crap. Which was funny considering the man was a walking equivocator. A liar on all counts.

An unapologetic heart breaker.

Total buttwipe... and the devil himself was going to freeze over before I let Gunner Steele handle my case.

After he'd stormed out, I'd made the decision that if Gunner was the one who showed up at my door in two hours, I'd hit the road. Yep, I'd rather risk my life than spend a second longer with '*Good-for-nothing-Gunner.*'

I'd paced the living room for a while, watching the clock tick, then convinced myself to do something to preoccupy my time until seven o'clock rolled around. I'd stepped into the marble, two-person shower and let the steaming water pound my shoulders for what felt like an hour. After that, I'd pulled on a pair of jeans and a Steele Shadows hoodie that Shepherd—or was it Wolf?—had sent over. To my shock, everything fit, even the furry little hiking boots that had to be a couple of hundred bucks. Not that I was surprised. From the moment I pulled up to their mansion, I realized the rumors of the Steele fortune weren't rumors at all. The guys were loaded. Millionaires? No, *billionaires*, the story went. That luxurious lifestyle carried over into Cabin 3, my little refuge. All cherry oak hardwood floors, buttery-soft leather couches over rich Chinese rugs. A kitchen with copper cookware and upscale appliances. The space was warm and welcoming, with the massive stone fireplace that rivaled any vacation cabin.

Except this was no vacation, this was a place where people went to escape.

I stared out the windows at the canvas of oranges, yellows, reds, the picturesque colors of fall that colored the soaring mountains. Beautiful, magical, peaceful. The opposite of what I was feeling.

Escape.

I couldn't believe I was one of those people. An *escapee*. Someone who needed protection. Someone who needed *others* to protect her.

My life had been completely flipped onto its head. I didn't know what tomorrow would bring. Heck, I didn't know what the next hour would bring.

And that feeling hit all too close to home.

My sister and I grew up in a small, two bedroom, one bathroom apartment in the Bronx, to a single mother who worked two jobs to make ends meet. A school librarian during the day, a waitress at night. If not for the charity of the cook—who had a shameless crush on my beautiful mother—there would have been nights we didn't eat at all. My dad walked out on us when we were toddlers. Another woman. Last I heard he was on his second child, second DWI, and facing jail time. My sister pretty much raised me from birth while taking care of herself on top of that. No hard feelings for my mom, though, she was only doing what she had to do to make the most of her situation. My mom worked every second that she was awake, if not at the library or diner, she was knitting scarfs to sell at the street corner on the weekends. It wasn't until I was a bit older that I realized how hard she really worked. I looked at her as a woman, not just a mom. A woman who got things done. She'd had my love since my first breath, and my respect years later.

My sister and I learned very early that we not only needed to take care of ourselves at home, but on the streets, too. My first mugging was when I was eight years old. Masked bastard didn't only take my measly allowance, he also took the rainbow purse my mom had knitted for me a week earlier. At my urging, the next day, my sister and I enrolled in a free community self-defense class. After that, we walked to school with our heads on a swivel. That was pretty much how our childhood went. After high school my sister and I took very different paths. Sarah went on to become a bartender, while I received a full scholarship to college and graduated with honors.

On my twenty-third birthday I received a call that mom had been in a head-on collision and died instantly. Two days after that, Sarah decided she needed to go "find herself." She left our apartment in the Bronx and moved down south where she bartended her way around from town to town. This lasted years.

Three months after mom had died, I'd discovered that my boyfriend of four years had been cheating on me. Hard to deny when I walked in on him with a swath of blonde hair bobbing between his legs. In a move I wasn't particularly proud of, I'd flung the Italian dinner I'd had in my hands into the back of the blonde's head—the dinner I'd made him as an 'I'm sorry I've been so distant since my mom died' dinner—then grabbed their bottle of cheap red wine and chugged it as I breezed out. Two days and the most brutal hangover later, a recruiter from Astor Stone approached me. Fate? Kismet? Whatever it was, I accepted the job on the spot and dove in with both feet working dawn until dusk. Honoring my hard-working mother? An escape from the pain? Didn't matter. I refocused my grief to my new goal of working my way up at Astor Stone. Everything else came second. A far second.

Including my love life.

For the last three years I'd been on a grand total of four dates.

Four.

Okay, fine—and one brutal, utterly humiliating drunken one-night-stand that still made me cringe. Who would've thought someone could vomit while orgasming?

Him. Not me.

Two of those dates had been set up by Kara. True to form, both were sculpted athletes, tanned and beautiful, with muscles as dense as tree trunks, and brains to match. Try discussing current events with someone who compared the latest loss of his favorite football team to 9/11. I'd switched to straight whiskey after that.

The other two men had asked me out like nice southern gentlemen. Except one was married. The other still lived with his mom.

Yep, that pretty much summed up my love life.

I was contemplating the disaster of my life when the growl of an engine pulled my attention away from the window.

Seven o'clock.

I jogged to the front door and craned my neck as an ATV rolled to a stop.

Gunner Steele stepped out.

My groan was so loud I wondered if he'd heard it because his eyes instantly met mine through the window as he stepped onto the porch.

Boom, boom, boom.

If sarcasm had a knock, that was it. I rolled my eyes and opened the door.

"Thanks for knocking this time."

"Thanks for answering."

Fresh from the shower, sunlight shimmered off the gold highlights in his wet, brown hair. Shaggy, with just enough length to remind the world he didn't give a damn. As if his tattoos and attitude didn't already do that. A worn, black leather jacket hung over a snug grey T-shirt that had me wondering what he looked like without it. Jeans and cowboy boots completed the ultimate bad boy look.

"You ready?"

My gaze snapped back up to his, those penetrating dark irises focused only on me.

"You're really taking my case?"

"If I think you need protection after hearing your story, yes."

"And you're the one who's going to be my bodyguard?"

"Take it or leave it. But I promise you, I will not have this discussion again."

My gaze shifted over his shoulder to the ATV, fighting an internal battle in my head. I needed protection, I knew that much to be a fact. I could tough out a few days with Gunner Steele. I also told myself that I would not be hypnotized by the man's body. Or that face.

Or those eyes.

After all, look where that got my sister.

"Where're we—"

"Grab a coat." He turned and started down the steps.

I snatched a Steele Shadows Security jacket from the coat rack and followed him outside.

"Get in." He slid behind the wheel of the ATV.

I pulled on the jacket—a few sizes too big—and ducked into the ATV. "I thought we were having our meeting right now. You know, to go over why I'm here."

"We are. Busy day." He handed me a brown bag. "Breakfast on the go."

I blinked, now *this* surprised me. A thoughtful gesture from '*Good-for-nothing-Gunner?*' An olive branch perhaps? I opened the bag and my mouth watered—a sausage, egg, cheese biscuit with a side of hash browns. Fresh, wrapped in foil. Not fast food. Someone had made these, in a real kitchen. Did Gunner cook? Did Gunner cook for *me*?

"Thank you," I forced out.

He nodded to a mug in the cupholder that read *Boob Man*. "Coffee."

"Thanks." I let the *Boob Man* slide.

No response.

He took off down a lighted, manicured trail, the early morning sunlight slanting through the trees like golden spears. Although the morning was cold, I was surprisingly comfortable in the jacket.

I sipped my coffee. "Where are we going?"

"Perimeter check."

"Perimeter check?"

A quick dip of his chin in response—a "yes," apparently.

"Of what?"

His brow furrowed. "The perimeter."

I rolled my eyes. "Of what? The perimeter of *what?*"

This guy and his communication skills. Or lack thereof, I should say.

"The property."

I blinked. "Don't you guys own, like, the entire mountain?"

"A bit more."

So this was going to take a while. Resigning to the fact that small-talk was not Gunner's forte, I pulled breakfast from the bag, realizing I hadn't eaten a thing since the peanuts on the plane ride from Aruba.

There was only one muffin.

I frowned, looked at him. "Aren't you going to—"

"Not hungry."

Okay dokey, then. I stared at the wrapped heaven on my lap, a twinge of insecurity creeping up. Eat—*ravage*—the breakfast while the man next to me ate nothing and watched? Then, an even more unsettling thought came over me... the fact that I cared. Something you should know about me is that I love food. *Good* food. There was only one thing that kept me, Lexi York, from eating with gusto... and that was when I was attracted to the man I was with.

Curve ball.

Dammit, dammit, dammit, was all I could think. Of *ALL* the freaking guys.

So in some warped attempt to punish myself for having feelings other than total disdain for Gunner, and also to ensure he didn't find me attractive, I ripped open the muffin and bit into the thing like a grizzly bear would attack its prey. Crumbles fell from my chin onto my lap.

And it felt good.

Damn good.

Chomping like a Clydesdale, I glanced out of the corner of my eye and swear I saw the corner of Gunner's lip curl up. I washed the bite down with a hefty gulp of coffee—and scalded my throat, inciting a coughing fit that included cannon-like spurts of half-chewed biscuit shooting out of my mouth.

Yep, I'd definitely just ensured that Gunner Steele didn't find me the least bit attractive.

Good.

It was for the best.

"You alright?" He slowed the ATV.

"Yeah." Tears streamed down my face as I wiped my mouth with my sleeve. "Hey, next time you bring a gal coffee, might want to tell her that it just came off the boiler."

"Next time you need to prove to yourself you don't mind eating in front of a guy, try sipping first."

My brow cocked and I shot him my best *seriously?* look even though my cheeks flushed with embarrassment.

Pondering if Gunner Steele might be more intuitive than I thought, I took another bite, this one a bit less rabid.

We took a curve, then veered off the trail in the woods. Sunlight sparkled through the colorful trees. Leaves scattered the forest floor where the underbrush appeared to be trimmed and cleaned out. The Steele brothers took pride in their property, and based on their chiseled exteriors, I guessed they did all the manual labor themselves.

I'd moved onto the hash brown when Gunner had decided I was taking too long to eat and began our meeting.

"Alright, let's start from the beginning," he said, scanning the fences. "Tell me what brought you to Steele Shadows. At four in the morning."

After taking a *careful* sip of coffee, I began.

"Astor Stone hired me ten years ago as an office assistant, where I worked my way up to an intern as an agent."

"You bullied your way up."

"What's that supposed to mean?"

"You didn't get promoted. You found out what the company really does and you bargained for a shot."

"How do you know what Astor does?"

He shot me a quizzical look and a few puzzle pieces clicked together. I knew Astor Stone hired outside help for security detail, and no one was better at security than Steele Shadows. They must've hired Gunner at some point.

"What makes you think I bullied my way up?"

"Because Astor doesn't hire office assistant to be agents. His team is primarily made up of former military or government guys."

"Maybe I am."

He snorted at this.

"Anyway, I was given one shot at an undercover gig, and..." I looked down, my stomach clenching.

"And let me guess, your cover was blown and they've hung you out to dry."

"In a nutshell, yes."

I couldn't even look at the guy. I exhaled and focused on the sunrise as I launched into the story of how I failed my undercover assignment of observing a man suspected of being a Russian spy. I told him of me stumbling onto Bear in Aruba and getting thrown into an incident that involved me fighting for my life and killing his two main bodyguards. It appeared that Aruban authorities were pursuing the angle that the incident was a 'strip club drug deal gone bad.' Apparently, both Sausage Gut and Shifty were known drug dealers and gang bangers in the area. As far as I know, there was no international manhunt for me. At least I had that going for me. My stomach rolled as I told Gunner how my purse and cell phone had been left behind—that Bear had not only my personal information but also access to confidential emails from Astor Stone. Unless Bear was stupid, he'd come after me for four reasons. One, I'd killed his pals, two, I could point out every one of his cronies in a lineup, three, to torture me for information that Astor Stone had on him and his crew. And four, the scariest of the possibilities, that he would hold me as ransom until Astor Stone told the government that Bear and his pals were *not* suspected of foreign espionage.

Other than the subtle shift of his head as he searched the fence line, Gunner didn't move a muscle, didn't ask a question, simply listened.

"So, I traded my earrings for a Chevy and drove here." I blew out a breath. "Listen, I just need a place to go until I can figure stuff out. I can't go home, or anywhere they'd expect me. So, here I am." I looked at him. "I understand you set people up with fake identities, right?"

A few seconds passed as he continued to stare straight ahead, the sharp lines of his face pulling in deep thought and something else resembling anger.

"What's this guy's name again?" He finally asked.

"Sergei Orlov. Known as Bear."

"And the government thinks he's a Russian spy, operating here in the US?"

"Well it's our job to confirm that suspicion but yes, that's why we were hired to look into him."

"When did he go dark?"

"Two weeks ago."

"Where does he live?"

"Has houses all over the country. He owned a successful tech company before selling his shares and going dark."

"Where are his houses?"

"All over. Has a place in New York, Colorado, ranch in Wyoming, I think—"

"Do you have his file?"

"No... no, all that's in my laptop. No doubt Astor has restricted my access by now."

A minute passed with me wondering why he was focusing only on Bear.

"Does the name Knight Fox mean anything to you?" He asked.

"Knight Fox?"

"Yes."

"It doesn't ring a bell."

"Do you remember the names of his associates?"

"I've been taking notes at the cabin..." I stopped and looked at him, his shoulders tense, his knuckles white against the wheel.

Thanks to my sister, I knew Gunner's father, Duke Steele, had been top dog at the NSA for many years. His death had made national news. A heart attack, so they'd said, but in my circle at Astor Stone, I'd heard rumors that his sons believed their father had been murdered. I also knew that his brother was fighting for his life after a failed suicide attempt.

Failed? Or attacked like his father?

And was this *Knight Fox* the suspected culprit?

Was it possible that Gunner thought Bear was somehow connected to his family drama?

Or... did Gunner think Sergei Orlov *was* the Knight Fox? It would make sense considering the barrage of questions that had absolutely nothing to do with *me*, or my protection.

If there was one thing I already knew about Gunner Steele it was that he didn't back down. If Gunner thought Bear was the one who attacked his family, the two-hundred and fifty-pound Russian was as good as dead.

... And this presented me with an interesting opportunity.

If Gunner Steele could help me track down Bear, I could deliver the Russian to Astor, redeem myself, and get my job back—and probably a promotion on top of that.

I just had to figure out a way to work with the bulldozing jerk, for him to *let* me work with him. To do that, I needed him to like me. Or, at least think that I didn't hate him. Sneaky? Underhanded? Perhaps. Payback for what he did to my sister? Absolutely. Kill two birds with one stone? I could do that.

But a haunting question gnawed at me. If Gunner and I were able to track down Bear, would I be able to get to Bear before Gunner put a bullet between the Russian's eyes?

9

GUNNER

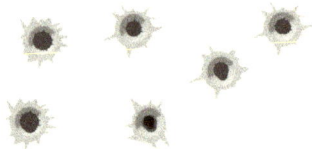

"*I* need you to pull everything you can on Sergei Orlov, aka, Bear."

The soda sloshed from Wolf's hands. He kicked his heels off the desk and sat up in his chair.

"Shit, Gunn, you scared me."

"Sergei Orlov." I crossed the darkened room that housed our security system. Dozens of television screens, monitors and computers flashed across the room. As head of security, it was Wolf's second home.

A home that he'd apparently fallen asleep in.

He flicked the soda off his shirt. "Who?"

"Former CEO of Eagle Technologies. Known as Bear."

"Okay, give a sec."

"Need it now, bro."

"Hang the hell on." Wolf grabbed a wad of used napkins from the trashcan and began dabbing himself off. I grabbed the can from his hand and set it down.

"Who the hell drinks Coke at eight in the morning?"

"Someone who's been up since one, dude."

I took a second to think about the last time I'd slept. Yesterday? The day before? How long, even?

Satisfied with his shirt, Wolf sat up started logging into his computer. "Okay, Sergei Orlov. What's going on?"

"Orlov is suspected of being involved in a Russian spy ring here in the US."

Wolf's brows shot up. "You serious?"

"Yep. Born and raised here, started a tech company, made a boatload of money, then went dark."

"What do you mean *went dark?*"

"Fell off the map. Sold his shares and no one's heard of him again."

"You think he's the Knight Fox?"

"That's exactly what you're going to find out."

"Okay, give me everything you've got."

"That's it."

His fingers lifted from the keyboard. "That's *it?*"

"Yep."

Wolf blew out an exasperated breath. "Okay... I've got his name—assuming it's real, by the way—his nickname, his company's name. I can work with this."

"Word is he owns a lot of property across the US. Can you pull those addresses?"

"You're wanting to know if he has a house around here?"

"Well, you're pretty adamant that the Knight Fox was, or still is, here in Berry Springs, right?"

"Yes. To review, your dad rogue, researching the assassination of a high ranking Russian official. He was killed after hacking into emails belonging to the Russian that were signed by KF—the Knight Fox respectfully—and determined that those emails were sent from here in Berry Springs. He went digging around where he shouldn't have, and got killed for it."

"Dad never did like red tape. What about the shell company? You confirmed the link with Berry Springs, too, right?"

"Yes, I found a bank account where deposits of millions of dollars aligned with big time assassinations around the world, including your dad's. I traced that money to Russia, and back to another shell company that links here, to Berry Springs. So, yeah, I think it's safe to assume the Knight Fox lives here, or is here now, at least."

"And I want you to find out if Bear has been here within the last few years."

"I can look for properties under his name and his company's name but remember, if he's a Russian spy, the guy probably has more covers than a CIA agent. His properties could be under different names, the works."

"You not up for the challenge, dude?"

"One, fuck you. Two, wanna take a shot at this yourself, genius?"

As much as I wanted to punch him in the face at that moment, I knew that no one on the planet—aside from my dad—was as good at hacking into systems as Wolf Blackwood. The guy was a computer genius. A cocky computer genius but genius nonetheless.

He took my silence as resignation of his offer, and continued, "I'm saying that this might be a boots-on-the-ground mission as much as me hacking into it. The fact that we have a unique nickname is a big deal. We can start by talking to the employees that were closest to Bear at his tech company. Then, find his hangouts, his restaurant, favorite bars, where he grocery shopped, where he took a shit. See if anyone has seen Bear, or someone called the Knight Fox."

I nodded, my thoughts spinning. Wolf wasn't only a computer genius, he was one heck of a detective.

"Where did you get this info, anyway?" He asked.

"Cabin 3."

"No kidding? How does she know about it?"

"The company she worked for—Astor Stone. She was assigned undercover to Bear's case, then got exposed. They knew she was undercover."

He frowned and looked up. "Well, if I were you, I'd look into everyone at Astor Stone, too. How did this Bear guy know who she was? Maybe he's got someone on the inside there, or maybe he blackmailed someone. In which case, all you have to do is give me a few bits of info about that person and we can also blackmail them for everything they know about the guy."

"You're an evil genius, Wolf."

"Why you hired me. ... And, you have no idea, Gunn." Wolf chuckled, then tilted his head to the side. *"Or*, maybe your girl is somehow involved in this whole thing. Ever thought about that?"

"First off, she's not my girl."

"First off, you wouldn't have jumped at that so quickly if you hadn't thought about it." He wiggled his eyebrows. "Bet you could draw those curves on this piece of paper, right now, with your eyes closed." He slid a pen in front of me. "Eh? You could, huh?"

I tossed the pen into the dartboard across the room. Bullseye.

Wolf laughed. "Second, I mean, what are the odds she's *here?* Now? That's all I'm saying. We already agreed that the Knight Fox, or anyone associated with him, could be *any*where. *Anyone, anywhere."*

I paused. Why did I automatically assume the woman didn't have something up her sleeve? What the hell was wrong with me?

In an effort to regain my ballsac, I squared my shoulders and said, "Check into her, too, then. I want to know everything about her."

"Wise move. Ever figure out what her deal with you is?"

"Don't know and don't care. Probably pissed off someone she knows."

"Well that reach is far and wide, bro."

I snorted, then stilled because it was true.

Wolf spun his chair and faced the computers. "Anyway, I'll get on this right away. It would go a lot faster if I could get a list of employees of both Eagle Tech and Astor Stone. Maybe you can get that info from your girl. Oops, I mean Cabin 3—"

"Lexi."

"Lexi? That's her name? What? She come in straight off the pole?"

"Not all women whose name ends in *xi* are strippers, Wolf." I cocked my head. "Had a dog named Lexi once." Damn good one too.

He laughed at this, then said, "Trixi, Pixi, Maxi, Dixi... pretty sure that sums up where my savings account disappeared to after leaving the Marines."

"And look what you've got to show for it. A nice family, a pair of strapping twin boys, one of those white fences that women always say they want..."

His face squeezed in disgust—because having a family was as top of mind for Wolf as his next prostate exam. He grinned. "Just missing the puppy named Lexi."

I snorted and glanced out the window. Somehow, I was pretty sure both Wolf and I would be on the floor missing our left nut if Lexi heard the last thirty-seconds of our conversation.

. . .

... If she was who she said she was, anyway.

10

GUNNER

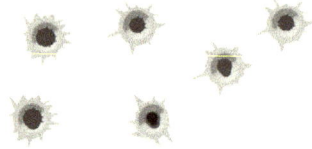

I muttered a few choice curse words as I glanced at my watch—already two minutes late for a Steele Shadows conference call I was supposed to be leading.

Shit, fuck, *goddammit.*

I jogged to my bedroom and slid behind the makeshift office I'd set up in front of the windows. Although there were plenty of spare rooms in the house I could have used, the thought of setting up an official office for myself meant not only that I was assuming Feen wasn't going to pull through, it also meant that I was accepting this new life for myself. The freaking CEO of a multi-million dollar company. Gunner Steele, a businessman. Gunner Steele, wielder of emails and P&L statements instead of AK 47's and KA-BARs.

Fuck. That.

Throw me in the middle of any war zone and I was as comfortable as a baby suckling a tit. Throw me at the head of a table in a board room and I become a blubbering mess. I'd rather remove each of my eyes with plastic spoons. Meetings, conference calls, reports, taxes, deadlines. It wasn't only that I hated it, it was that it wasn't *ME*.

And the worst part about that? Everyone knew it. Everyone knew I wasn't cut out for business.

Everyone was expecting me to fall on my face.

And the saddest part about that was, I was, too.

The thing was, I couldn't. I couldn't fail. I couldn't ruin what my father had built and what Feen was so proud to take over.

So there I was, dialing into a conference call about something about something, where I was about to dictate orders about something.

What. The. *Fuck.*

Several beeps, some torturous small talk and a roll call later, the pre-scheduled weekly update began.

"I'll begin. This is Madd, with the Colorado office."

Madd, short for Maddox, was a retired Army Ranger we'd recruited to lead our Denver office where we had five staff, including himself.

"We've just signed on a new case. A sixteen year old up-and-coming pop star who came home to naked pictures of herself smeared with semen."

"Classy." A smartass chimed in.

Madd continued, "I've agreed to take her into one of our safe houses until police get the DNA results back and nail the guy."

"So a few days, tops?" I asked.

"Hopefully. She's got Dog running around like crazy. Wants different sheets, organic food, the works." Madd cleared his throat. "Speaking of Dog..." there was a pause that had my back straightening. "We got our routine drug tests back yesterday afternoon... Dog's came back positive for weed."

My grip tightened around the phone. Dog was another Army recruit who I'd trained personally. The kid was from the wrong side of the tracks who'd straightened his life out. Became one hell of an operative. And a damn good guy.

"What the fuck, Madd?" I ignored a gasp somewhere on the phone. "Weren't you checking in with him? Watching him?"

"Am I supposed to babysit Dog along with my other clients, Mr. Steele?"

The name stung but the tone was like a knife in my gut. Then, everything—the lack of sleep, food, patience—came barreling through my system in the form of white hot anger.

"Fire him."

"What?"

"You heard me, Madd. Fire him. We have a strict no drug policy here at Steele Shadows Security. Every single one of us has to have routine drug testing. Every single one of us signed on the dotted line. Dog broke the rules. Dog's out."

"Mr.—"

"Gunner."

" ... Gunner, I'd like you to reconsid—"

"I'll reconsider your role if you question me again, Maddox. Our mission is to serve and protect. Other people's lives depend on it. On *us*. No drugs is our policy. He's out."

"Gunner, your dad would put him on probation, and then—"

"I am *not* my father!" I exploded into the phone. Then, like a spoiled child, slammed down the receiver, ending my portion of the call.

After punching the desk to punctuate that I was, indeed, an unprofessional, childish, unrestrained asshole, a small voice called out from the doorway.

"Sir?"

I spun around to see our head housekeeper, Opal, standing in the doorway. The woman had helped raise me since I was a baby. Instead of her usual soothing, calm expression topped off with colorful dreadlocks, that day, after seeing my outburst, she looked at me not with fear, but a sadness. Pity. I would have preferred fear, to be honest. She was yet another woman I'd let down.

Opal took a small step into the room, hands clasped at her front. "I've been asked to remind you that your shift at the hospital starts in an hour."

I looked at the clock.

Shit, shit, shit.

"Thanks, Opal."

She scurried away.

I buried my head in my hands.

I had less than an hour to make a dent in the hundreds of unread emails glaring at me. After that blessed event? An ice-cold four hours of counting tiles in the ICU.

The sun had just set by the time I rolled into the garage. I was tired, hungry, and had spent the entire day in a cloud of general pissed-offedness.

After playing CEO, I'd driven straight to the hospital to relieve Ax from his shift of watching over Phoenix in the ICU. From there, I'd met Gage in the woods, where he and several of our staff were still combing the woods for Celeste, which turned up nothing. Nothing, nada, zilch. My already non-existent patience was waning. Especially when I'd told Ax I was going to swing by the police station on my way home to light a fire under the blues' asses, to which he replied, 'hell no, you're not.' Apparently, he'd heard about the conference call earlier and decided my leadership skills were having an *off* day. Fine. Fan-*fucking*-tastic. Like I gave a damn.

I slid off my bike and stalked across the garage. There was only one thing that calmed me when I was that restless—a few solo hours in the range. Bypassing the house, where I knew I'd face a firestorm of questions from Dallas about the conference call, I traded my Harley for a four-wheeler and took off into the darkening evening.

Steele Shadows had two shooting ranges, one indoor and one outdoor. Phoenix had established a rule about no outdoor shooting after dark after an unfortunate incident with our neighbor, old man Erikson, and a poorly timed ricochet. Damn thing blew the hunting cap right off his bald head. He was in an uproar while I was in stitches. Teach him to wander around our property at night.

I pulled up to the long, metal building that sat below the main house.

Pop, pop, pop!

The muffled sound of gunshots told me I wasn't the only one in need of blowing off some steam. I took note of the golf cart parked to the side, then pushed through the front door and scanned the room. The first thing that surprised me was the lack of music blaring through the systems. The second was that the building was mostly dark, with only a dim light over the last stall. A single spotlight illuminated a target with the center blown to smithereens.

Not bad.

Pop... pop!

A few more shots, this one to the right of the center.

I crossed the concrete floor, glancing in each stall until I came to the end.

My brows shot up.

Wearing shooting glasses and noise-cancelation

earmuffs that were two sizes too big, Lexi York was armed, ready, and laser-focused on her target. A grin tugged at my lips as I stepped back, out of sight of her peripheral.

More shots, this time, left of center.

I skimmed her shooting stance, the hug of her worn Levi's, the way the Steele Shadows sweatshirt swamped her body, hiding her curves like a mask only making me want to see more. Her fuzzy eskimo boots from earlier had been traded with a pair of flip flops. Freshly painted pink toenails sent a rush of blood to my cock and my mind wondering what it would be like to have them in my mouth. Her brown hair was down, falling around her shoulders in a wavy mess that had me picturing what she looked like after a roll in the sack. Something about that body, that face, those big ass earmuffs combined with the gun in her hand had my pants tightening like a pre-teen in sex-ed class.

Not cool.

This insta-fantasy was topped off by the half-drunk bottle of microbrew sitting on the bench next to her.

A woman with a gun and a fancy import. Holy hell. Lexi York had checked off my two most important boxes right then and there.

I inhaled, calming the blood flow and forced myself to focus on her shots as she fired off a few more.

"You need to shift your focus."

The squeal that came out of her was ten octaves higher than when I'd caught her on the treadmill, although this time, she held a nine millimeter in her hand. She spun around, a shaky aim pointed directly between my eyes.

"Might want to rethink that, sweetheart."

Her arm dropped with her jaw. "You scared the *crap* out of me! What the heck are you doing? I could have shot you!"

"Not with that aim." I took the gun from her hands and reloaded.

"What's that supposed to mean?"

I checked the SIG p938 she'd chosen to shoot with. "Nice choice."

"Oh, well, thanks, Kemosabe, your approval means everything to me. I repeat, what's wrong with my aim?"

"You asked what's that supposed to mean."

"Are you always like this?"

"Charming, smooth-talking, charismatic?"

"Crude, crass, demanding."

"Yes."

"Lucky me."

"Step back."

She did as she was told—surprisingly—and I stepped up to the edge.

Pop, pop, pop! Three, right through the middle.

"... Wow. Not too ba—"

I sent the target back as far as it would go. Just for kicks, flicked the switch that turned the lane into a discotheque that included bursts of lights and lasers zipping across the target.

Pop, pop, pop! Target destroyed. I flicked off the light and reloaded.

"Show off." She stepped beside me.

I handed her the gun and nodded for her to get up to the plate.

"Who taught you to shoot?" I asked.

"Astor. Why?"

"You suck."

"You're an ass."

I was beginning to like the little attitude she had on her. I jerked my chin to the target, telling her to focus.

Despite the eye roll, she did as she was told, again—and I was beginning to like that too. Although I'd be lying if this sudden shift in demeanor didn't have me questioning her motives.

I pushed that thought aside. For the moment, anyway.

"Like I said, shift your focus. You're focusing on the target." I stepped closer. "Aim like you're about to shoot."

She raised the gun.

"Okay. There are three sights in your sight picture. Rear sight, front sight, and your target. Let me guess, you're focused on the center that I just blew out of that target?"

She grunted.

"And that's incorrect. Now, look down the barrel of your gun. The notch at the tip of the barrel is the front sight. The *U* closer to your nose is the back sight. An idiot aligns both those sights with their target, then shifts focus to the target and pulls the trigger. Don't do that. Align, then focus on the front sight *only*. Everything else should be blurry. Got it?"

A subtle nod.

"Your grip's also off, *Kemosabe*."

I shifted behind her and reached around her sides. Her shoulders tensed, her head raising slightly as my body pressed against hers.

"Relax, sweetheart." My nose followed a vanilla scent behind her ear like a bloodhound. I whispered, "I'm adjusting your stance."

I felt a shiver sweep over her, then her body slowly leaned into mine, that ass pressing up against my groin.

The blood funneled between my legs like a tornado.

"I'm not your sweetheart," she whispered in a sultry voice that sent my dick kicking.

"No, you're not," I pressed harder against her. "Because if

you were, you better believe I'd be showing you a different grip right now."

A flush colored her skin, the long, feathery lashes dipping over her bedroom eyes. Her cheek turned toward me, brushing my lips when...

"Heyoo!" Gage's voice boomed through the air as the front door flew open. The silence—and whatever the hell had just happened between us—was shattered by stomping boots and incessant chatter.

I dropped my hands and stepped back, willing the blood to rise back to my head. Heavy footsteps echoed down the lanes with the cocking of guns cracking in the background.

"Yo, Gunn, heard about the conference call. I really think —" Gage froze, locking on Lexi. "Whoops..." He glanced at me, a shit-eating grin smearing over his face. "Sorry. Didn't mean to interrupt. The boys and I were gonna shoot off a few before dinner, but, hey if you two want to be alone..."

Lexi looked at me, a twinkle in her whiskey eyes. "It's okay, they can stay. I don't think I'm quite ready for that grip lesson just yet, Mr. Steele."

I couldn't fight the grin. "Didn't think you were." I nodded back to the target. Okay, now, get back at it. Front sights. Go."

11

LEXI

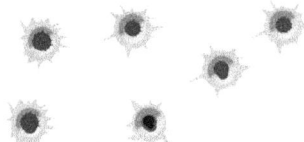

The low, deep voices behind me told me that whatever Gunner and his brother were talking about was not intended for my ears. So, as any good woman would do, I strained to listen. Their oldest brother, Phoenix, came up several times, as well as Celeste, a woman who'd gone missing. It wasn't until I heard *Bear* and *Knight Fox* several times that my suspicion that Gunner thought the Russian had something to do with his family's tragedies was confirmed.

There was a plan forming. I needed to figure out how to get in on it.

The chatter hushed and I could feel their eyes on me.

I focused on my front sights, as instructed, and tried to clear my mind of the moment that had happened between Gunner and I.

The guy was surprising me even more than my waffling thoughts about him. He was—as I'd been told—an insensitive jerk but that wasn't all he was. I'd seen glimpses of someone else, a tortured soul who was *trying*. Making an effort. One step forward after ten back. Trying to fix the broken mess of his family, trying to keep his head above water. Trying to become a better man?

Then, he went and pressed his body against mine. The electricity, the butterflies, the sheer lightning that had pulsed through my veins the second we touched was nothing less than jarring.

Despite my decline of his offer, my body *was* ready for that "grip lesson." It was that my brain wasn't. If his brother hadn't broken up the moment, I wondered if we would have kissed. More than that, if *I* would have kissed *him*. How would that have complicated things? Complicated my plan of using Gunner to find Bear, aka, the Knight Fox?

One thing was for certain, Gunner had an impact on me, a visceral want—a need—that was slowly simmering inside. There was an uncontrollable attraction between us that started at my toes and worked its way up to my jumbled brain.

I needed to take a step back, for three reasons. One, because I wasn't sure if I was strong enough to deny him. It had been over a year since I'd had sex and Gunner was a walking aphrodisiac, a force worthy of bringing any level-headed woman to her knees. Two, I knew his type. All too well. Taming a man like Gunner Steele was never going to happen. Men like him were never going to be a one-woman man. I had a hunch that if I got one taste of the man, there was no going back. Third, and perhaps most importantly, my sister would kill me. There was one sister code you didn't break. That was it.

I fired off a few more shots, releasing the frustration that was quickly mounting.

"Front." Gunner's sharp voice sounded behind me.

I shifted my focus to the front, then *bam*, bullseye. A few more shots, a few more bullseyes.

A whistle sounded from across the room, followed by a few heckles.

"Woooowie who let Annie Oakley in the room?"

"Nice shot, sweetheart."

"Damn, Gunn, you gonna let a girl beat you?"

I grinned and glanced over my shoulder. "Yeah, gonna let a girl beat you?"

He pulled the gun from his belt and stepped into the next lane.

"Ready to go dark?"

"Does it involve that grip of yours?" I asked before I could catch myself.

His gaze shifted to his buddies in the corner, then pinned me with an intensity that had the hair on my arms prickling. "I don't share, Lex."

"I don't answer to nicknames."

"We'll see about that." He winked, then flicked a switch and the range went dark.

More hoots and hollers, then the "discotheque" was flipped on. It was like a swirling funhouse of light, surely to mess with anyone's focus—gun in hand or not.

"First one to hit twenty bullseyes wins. Loser has to pick up the bullet shells."

I counted the handful at my feet. "Done."

"Not just there. In the entire building."

My eyes skirted around the concrete floors, the blinking lights flickering off of thousands of bullet shells.

"You're on, Big Shot. Let's—"

Before I could finish the sentence, Gunner took his first shot and... bullseye.

I sucked in a breath. Focusing on front sights, took my first shot—bullseye. Gunner dipped his chin in approval, then went back to shooting. We went back and forth like this, the blasts of the guns awakening a jittery, excited energy in me I hadn't felt in a while. A mischievous spark that was signaling every sexual sensor in my body.

I noticed Gunner's shots had slowed indicating that he was *letting* me win. I didn't care, though, because there was no way I was going to spend the evening picking up bullet shells, especially considering that I was starving.

"New bet," I yelled.

He lifted his earmuffs.

"Loser has to make dinner."

The guy hit his ten remaining bullseyes—in a freaking row—and kicked my butt.

"Seriously?" I ripped off my earmuffs.

"I don't cook unless it involves biscuits and bacon. Or, BLT's. I can make a mean BLT. Steele family favorite."

"Confession. I don't cook either. Which probably surprises you." I motioned to my hips and instantly regretted it. Damn insecurities.

He cocked his head and skimmed my body with a heat that matched the one settling in between my legs.

"I don't believe you can't cook."

"What? Because I'm a woman I'm supposed to whip up a four course meal wearing nothing but an apron and six-inch heels?"

"Exactly."

I shook my head. "Caveman."

"Apron or not—although I prefer not—this caveman is hungry. Come on." He holstered his gun.

After a few more whistles and needling from the jarheads, we stepped outside. Night had fallen. Not a star in the sky, not a sliver of a moon. Only a swift, cool breeze scented with rain. I wrapped my arms around myself.

"Storm's coming tonight." Gunner grabbed a camo

Carhartt from the back of his ATV and wrapped it around my shoulders.

"Thanks," I felt my cheeks heat as we looked at each other. I forced myself to take a step back. "So. Where am I whipping up this four course dinner?"

"Depends. Apron or not?"

"Apron."

"Then we'll grab something."

"Really?"

"Yeah, I don't want to wait an hour on PB&J's." He winked. "You too classy for BBQ?"

I glanced down my oversized hoodie, jeans that fit too tight, and flip flops. "Think I'll fit right in."

"Good. Hop in."

"But my golf cart—"

"I'll handle it."

I slid into the ATV and we drove up the hill to the main house. I was in awe of the mansion ahead of us, all lit up with lights. It was stunning. So unfitting of the man next to me. I couldn't put my finger on it but Gunner didn't fit in with the Steele brothers' opulent lifestyle. A small fishing cabin on a lake, or a hunting cabin on the tip of the mountain, *that* I could see. Thousands of square feet with butlers and maids, I couldn't.

He cut me a glance and as if reading my thoughts, said, "We inherited it."

And then it hit me, Gunner not only didn't fit in with this family, he was embarrassed by their wealth. The layers that were Gunner Steele continued to peel and my heart continued to soften.

"My childhood apartment could fit in your foyer."

"Where's that?"

"The Bronx."

"So that's where you got your love of guns."

"Oh, nice cliché, *jerk*."

"I'm joking."

"You're not entirely off, though, especially the area I grew up. Not for the faint of heart, or, overachievers, for that matter."

"You got a job at one of the most prestigious investigation companies in the country."

"Just because you grow up poor doesn't mean you can't make something of yourself."

He stared at me for a moment. "Tell me about that tattoo on your arm."

"You mean Lola?"

"You name your tattoos?"

"You don't?"

"There's not enough letters in the alphabet. Tell me about Lola."

My hand rubbed my bicep. "It's for my mom."

He looked over. "And?"

I cleared my throat. Although it had been years since she'd been gone, it was still difficult to talk about. "She was the hardest working woman I've ever met in my life. Single mom. She rose above her environment to make the most for me and my sister; she made the most of her situation. Reminded me of Rosie the Riveter. Mom knitted every second that she wasn't working." I yanked up my sleeve and pointed to the ball at her feet. "And she was beautiful. Stunning."

I felt his gaze boring into me.

"Anyway, Astor told me I'd have to have it removed if I wanted to be a special agent."

"Makes sense. It's identifiable."

"Guess it doesn't matter anymore." I exhaled the bad energy away. "Okay, tell me about yours."

"Which one?"

I skimmed his bare arms, rippled under a kaleidoscope of colors.

"Let's go with that vintage car."

"Oh you mean Rose?"

"Rose? So you do name your tattoos?"

"No, I name my cars."

We pulled into a massive garage that looked more like a showroom at a dealership.

"Holy *crap,* Gunner." My mouth dropped.

"I know…" He glanced down. Again, embarrassed. "My brothers like their toys."

My eyes rounded as I looked around the garage. Four meaty, mean-looking Harleys with all the bells and whistles. Three blacked-out, brand-new Chevy trucks. A Hummer. A cherry red Porsche, an electric yellow BMW Nazca, two G Wagons… and off in the corner, a vintage red, Ford Mustang, and a dented, rusted GTO sitting next to an even older mint green station-wagon-looking car. Tools, empty beer cans and Gatorade bottles scattered that area of the otherwise pristine garage.

"Well," I looked at Gunner and tilted my head. "Three are not like the others."

He snorted.

"Let me guess, those are yours."

He nodded. "I like cars. Like to work on them."

"Are one of these Rose?" I nodded to his arm.

"No." He cleared his throat. "I donated her."

My brows raised. "But you loved her enough to get her tattooed on your arm. Tell me."

He began tinkering with the ATV. "She was my first

restoration. Guess you could say she taught me the value of making good with what you've got."

No, Gunner Steele was nothing like his brothers.

"Where did she go?"

He didn't say anything for a minute. "To one of my buddies."

"Care to elaborate?"

He blew out a breath as if it pained him to tell an actual story. "A family came to us a few years back for protection. The fifteen year old boy—Ben—was getting bullied at school and the mom wanted us to teach him self-defense. She was even considering changing her name and starting over somewhere. It was bad. He was beaten up more than a few times. Put in the hospital once." The muscles in his jaw twitched. "Turned out, the kid was suicidal... So I worked with him, for weeks. He decided to give school one more shot and on his sixteenth birthday, he rolled up in a 1963 Aston Martin worth seven-figures."

"Rose."

A swift nod. "After graduating, he enlisted in the military. One of the best snipers we've got. Later, he donated the car to pay for a trauma unit at the local children's hospital. Wanted to keep the 'good' going, or so he said." Gunner paused. "Rose changed my life, Ben's, and hundreds of others. She didn't need to be discarded and replaced with the latest and greatest, she just needed to be given the love and elbow grease she deserved."

My heart kicked. I tore my gaze away from him in fear that I'd walk over and plant a kiss on his lips. A second passed in silence.

"What's the green one? I like it."

"Limited edition 1952 Hudson Hornet."

"She's beautiful."

"You should have seen her when I got her."

"You fix them up all by yourself?"

His gaze met mine. "Just because I'm rich doesn't mean I have other people do everything for me." He turned and grabbed a helmet from a rack. "Hope you don't mind helmet hair."

"We're taking your Harley to get food?"

"I've only got a few more weeks of riding time before it gets too icy. Scared?"

"Kind of."

His smile curved like a mischievous little devil. "I won't go too fast." He plucked a helmet from the wall and secured it to my head. I found myself wondering how many women had worn that helmet.

"It's Dallas's," he said, once again reading my thoughts. "She rides sometimes."

"Oh."

He grabbed the ends of my jacket, yanking me to him, his eyes locking on mine. My breath caught.

"Gets chilly." He pulled the zipper closed.

Not next to you, I thought.

I slid behind Gunner on the Harley and wrapped my hands around his thick waist. The motor growled to life.

"Tighter," he demanded, yanking my arms further around him.

My body pressed against his and we took off into the night, the woods zooming past us as we barreled down the dirt road. Despite the cool wind that whipped around me, I was toasty warm. I assumed it had everything to do with the guy I was holding onto. The vibration between my legs, the heat between us, that bad-boy feeling of danger that comes with being on the back of a man's bike. It was exhilarating. A smile caught me and I realized I wasn't only having fun being the girl on the back of Gunner Steele's bike, I was happy. For that fleeting moment, slicing through the night, the wind whipping around me, I was having fun. Careless, bad-decision fun.

The best kind.

My bliss was short lived when Gunner checked his phone. He veered onto the dusty shoulder and cut the engine. My pulse was still pounding when the silence settled around us.

"What's wrong?"

"Missed a call." He dialed and put the phone to his ear.

"How the heck did you hear it?"

"Had it on vibrate against my skin."

"That's responsible."

"That's having a brother in ICU."

I could hear both sides of the conversation as the call connected...

"Gunn, I'm knee deep in those little favors you asked me but there's something I found out that couldn't wait."

I recognized the voice from the guy who'd booked me in. Wolf, or Shepherd. Or Wolf?

"Talk." Gunner said.

"I've been able to pin a few of Bear's properties."

My stomach dropped.

Wolf continued, "You're not going to believe this. The Russian owns property here in Berry Springs."

"You're sure?"

"Yep. He's got some acres 'bout ten klicks from here. I checked the aerial view and it looks like it's got a barn on it. I think he leases the land to hunters."

"Any movement? You think he's there?"

"Could be."

"What's the address?"

"Texting now."

"Standby. I might need some backup."

"Thought you might. Let me know."

Click.

My pulse pounded as Gunner slid the phone back into his pocket.

"Looks like dinner is going to have to wait."

The engine roared to life.

"Wait, Gunner, maybe we should—"

Rocks flipped into the air as we peeled onto the road.

I grit my teeth and cursed. I had less than ten minutes to figure out how to deliver Bear's location to Astor.

I had less than ten minutes to come up with a plan to keep Gunner Steele from going to jail for capital murder.

12

LEXI

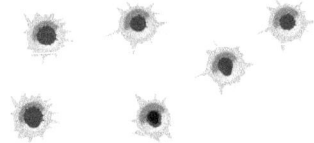

My nails dug into Gunner's sides, surely leaving marks. He didn't seem to notice and I didn't care.

We were flying down a pitted dirt road on his Harley, skidding around corners, each straight stretch taking us faster and faster. The guy was driving with blind aggression. Uncontrolled, unrestrained and I was along for the freaking ride. I was being dragged into a situation that was lose-lose, no matter what happened. There was no way I could connect with Astor at that moment—I didn't even have a cell phone—so my focus shifted to figuring out how to keep Bear alive.

How could I keep Gunner from killing the man he suspected of attacking his family? Killing his dad?

I needed Bear alive for two reasons. One, to get my job back. Two, to keep Gunner from spending the rest of his life behind bars. Because apparently, his well-being had become just as important to me.

The bike spun around a corner, sending my body sliding to the side and my heart leaping into my throat. I swear my life flashed before my eyes. I'd had enough. I pounded my fists into Gunner's back, my hands bouncing off as if I were hitting a refrigerator.

He sent a scowl over his shoulder, then refocused on the road, where, thankfully, the bike began to slow.

"What the hell do you think you're doing?" I screamed over the wind. "You're driving like a crazy man! Let me off this thing!"

He didn't.

"I said, *let me off!*"

I still don't know where I got the balls to do this, but as he slowed around a hairpin corner, I gripped his shoulders and hurled myself off the bike, tumbling into the ditch like a sack of potatoes. Two seconds later, two hands slid under my shoulders and heaved me into the air, my toes dangling above the dirt.

"What the *hell* are *you* doing?" Rage spilled from his dark eyes.

"Let me *down.*"

He growled, lowered me to the ground and jabbed his fingers through his hair.

"You can't do this, Gunner."

Sprinkles of rain dotted the dust around us, the soft pitter patter on fallen leaves like a haunting backtrack for the fighting brewing between.

"Do what, *exactly?*" Even through the darkness, I could see a fury behind his eyes, so hot that if I had any good sense, I would have zipped my lips and taken a few steps back.

Well, my good sense was all cashed out.

"You can't go in there, guns blazing, and kill the guy. You can't kill him, Gunner. He's not worth it!"

Gunner lunged toward me. I stumbled back, my back up against a tree.

My eyes popped.

He stopped, control touching his eyes for a split second. Restraint. He spun on his heel and began pacing. "God*dammit* Lexi!"

"You can't ruin your life by destroying his, Gunner."

"The guy has ruined my *family*, Lexi. Don't you get that? Ruin *my* life? You think I care? Ruin the life I can't fucking stand? The life where I wake up every single day wishing I was somewhere else, someone else?" He exhaled. "This is happening, Lexi. And you're either in or you're out. Right now. You're in or you're out."

"You wouldn't leave me here."

"Try me."

We stared at each other, frozen in time, one on the brink of destruction, the other torn between every emotion known to man.

I cracked first.

"Don't kill him, Gunner."

"In or out, Lex."

"Don't kill him, Gunner."

Thunder rumbled in the distance. I swiped a raindrop from my cheek, grabbed my helmet and stalked to the bike.

"You might be reckless beyond understanding, Gunner, but you're not going to kill *me*. You slow this damn bike down or I *will* stay right here."

It was a test, a deeper test than I cared to admit.

Would he leave me?

A solid minute slid by—two stubborn bullheaded train wrecks at the ends of their ropes.

"Get on."

I released the breath I'd been holding and slid onto the

back. Sure enough, he took off at a conservative speed, but I still wasn't sure who'd won that battle.

A few minutes later, we turned onto a narrow dirt road I wouldn't have even noticed otherwise. Sprinkles shimmered like diamonds through his headlight as it reflected off a silver gate, secured with multiple locks.

"This is it?"

"According to Wolf, yeah. Bear owns about a hundred acres past this fence."

I craned my neck to see over his shoulder. Woods, woods, more woods. Dark, creepy, haunting.

Gunner cut the engine and slid off the bike. He checked the locks, then stalked back to the bike and pulled off his leather jacket.

"Hope you can climb fences." He crammed his jacket into a leather side carry and pulled out a flashlight.

"Can't you blow the locks off or something?"

"This isn't a western, sweetheart, and not without alerting everyone in the woods of our arrival."

Good point. And I let the sweetheart slide... fine... I kind of liked it. He helped me off the bike and scowled down at my flip flops.

I shrugged. "Didn't expect a midnight hike."

He peered at my feet for a moment then seemed to decide something. He turned, squatted. "Get on."

"Get on what?"

"Me."

"You're joking."

"I'm not in the mood to deal with a broken ankle or a snake bite tonight."

My toes curled. "Snakes?"

"Yep. Big, mean, nasty ones."

I crawled onto his back, cursing myself for my stupid

insecurities as he stood. He helped me over the fence, then with me on his back, we stepped into the woods with only his Maglite guiding us. The rain was already beginning to pick up.

I yanked up my hood. "So what exactly are you looking for?"

"According to the text Wolf sent, there's a barn not far from this entrance."

"And we're just going to walk to the front door, knock, and ask to borrow some sugar? Why are you so sure he's there, anyway?"

"I'm not."

My heart sparked with hope. I wanted nothing more than to find Bear but not at the cost of Gunner's freedom. I was in the middle of devising a plan to throw us off path when Gunner suddenly clicked off the light and stopped cold. The woods around us went dark, the drum of the rain breaking the eerie silence.

"Why'd you stop?" I whispered, not quite sure why.

He lowered me off his back. "There's a structure seven yards to our east."

"How did you see that?"

He shook his head as if he didn't care to waste breath explaining. "I want you to stay right by my side. Stay quiet, you understand?"

I nodded.

"*Quiet*, Lexi, got it?"

"Yes, *yes*. Quiet. Got it."

"I want you to wait at the edge of the woods while I check out the barn. If you hear a gunshot, I want you to turn and run as fast as you can back to the bike."

"Gunner—"

"We're not doing that right now. If you hear a shot, turn and run. Got it?"

I looked over my shoulder. "But I don't know if I'll remem—"

"Yes you will. I marked our path. Follow the trees marked with a fresh X in the trunk."

"You marked them with a knife?"

"Yes."

"I didn't even notice... When did you—"

"Once you get to the bike, Ax will be there to pick you up."

"Your brother?"

"Yes."

"When did you arrange all this?"

He dismissed my question and I remembered Gunner's life was personal security. He and his brothers probably had a contingency plan for every situation under the sun.

"You'll be safe with Ax. He'll take care of you."

"What about you, Gunner? What about you?"

His eyes narrowed with an intensity that had my stomach dropping. "I'm going to end this. One way or another, I'm going to end this."

I knew there was no stopping the man. Nothing I was going to say or do was going to keep Gunner from storming that barn. So I followed him through the woods, stopping at the tree line as instructed.

Barely visible through the rain, a red barn stood in a small clearing, old, rotted, dilapidated. No lights, no cars. Nothing.

"Again, if you hear shots, go straight to the bike. Okay?"

I nodded.

With that, he turned away and slipped through the

clearing like a panther on the hunt. My heart raced as I watched him, the stealth, the speed, the confidence.

The carelessness.

Vengeance.

I hovered under a tree branch, shielding myself from the rain. I watched Gunner circle the barn, then, slip inside.

Seconds faded to minutes as I stood at my post, wide-eyed, on bated breath, waiting for him to come out.

Or, waiting to hear that gunshot.

It felt like standing on the edge of a ship in the middle of the ocean, waiting to fall.

What seemed like an hour passed, although I'm sure it was only a handful of minutes.

Nothing.

No movement, not a single sound. Only a barn, dark as night, sitting in the distance.

I looked over my shoulder, then turned back to the barn. Where was he? What had he found? What was taking him so long?

My tongue darted around my lips as my mind raced.

What if he was hurt?

I took another glance over my shoulder, then I did exactly what I was told not to. I darted out of the tree line, across the clearing and stumbled to the side of the barn. Chest heaving, I looked around and listened. Still nothing from inside. I waited until my pulse slowed, then ducked and jogged to the front door.

It was cracked open.

I grabbed a stick from the ground—a useless weapon that somehow made me feel less like a sitting duck.

I listened a few more beats, then slowly pushed open the door.

The gasp that escaped my lips was almost as loud as the

clatter of the branch slipping from my fingers and tumbling to the floor. The barrel of a gun slid between my eyes.

"*Shit.*" Gunner's voice broke the silence as he dropped the gun. My focus remained on the horror show in the center of the room.

"I told you to stay at the tree line," he snarled over drum of my heartbeat.

"That's *him.* That's Bear." The words came out in a breathy whisper.

"I thought so."

I crossed the dirty barn floor, forcing my jaw to close, and looked down at the two-hundred and fifty-pound Russian tied to a rickety wooden chair, with a single trail of blood running from the bullet hole in his forehead. His silky, blue button-up was saturated with blood and sweat stains. By the horrid scent of the room, I assumed his pants were saturated as well. His left eye was swollen shut. Dried blood colored his chin below a mouth that I guessed was missing its teeth.

"Holy *shit,*" I shook my head.

Gunner had turned his attention back to the window where he appeared to be checking the latch and frame. For prints, I assumed. Ignoring me, he stepped outside and I shifted my attention back to the dead man in front of me.

My gaze drifted down Bear's body to his hands, tied to the chair, each of his fingers shattered to a flattened, bloody pulp.

"They tortured him." I scanned his shoeless feet, marked with cuts and bruises.

"Then shot him like they did Phoenix." Gunner paused at the doorway, the rain pounding his shoulders.

I put my hands on my hips, my mind reeling. "So Bear isn't the one after your family." I stared at the man who was supposed to be my salvation, now sitting in a puddle of his own urine.

"No."

"Bear isn't the Knight Fox."

"How do you know about the Knight Fox?"

"I overhead you and your brother at the range."

His brow tipped up.

"Have you found any fingerprints?"

"No." He stepped inside.

"Anything at all?"

"Tracks outside."

"Vehicle?"

"Motorcycle."

"So either Bear arrived on a bike, which isn't likely, or his killer did." I nudged Bear's shin with my toe. "He hasn't been dead twenty-four hours."

"How do you know that?"

"He's in full rigor mortis. After twenty-four hours, the body goes back to a languid state."

A moment passed as we stared at the murdered man, the last thing we both expected to walk into.

"So, hang on," I frowned. "Bear and his crew were in Aruba, where he and I cross paths, then, what? He heads to Berry Springs where he gets schwacked in a barn?"

"Not five miles from where you sought refuge."

"You think he followed me to Berry Springs?"

"I don't think only to Berry Springs."

"You think he followed me to *Aruba,* too?"

"It fits. He knew who you were. It fits."

"No," I began pacing. "No, way. Kara, my friend, picked the location for our girls' trip, I had nothing to do with it." I started spinning. "And no one followed me to the airport after the attack, I'm sure of it. I'd even changed clothes, hair, everything. After I landed, I conned some man out of his truck. No. There's no way Bear knew all that."

"Lexi, if there's one thing I know about these guys it's that they have people everywhere. Bear knew you were onto him, very likely the entire time you worked in his office."

It was a jarring thought, one that sent my stomach swirling. Had I been in danger the entire time I'd been in Texas? More disconcerting than that, why hadn't I picked up on it?

I looked at Gunner. "Whoever did this inadvertently saved my life, then."

"No. Whoever did this killed my dad, tried to kill my brother, and kidnapped Celeste.

"It's all linked."

"And I have to figure out how. Let's go." He turned and started across the room.

"Wait, we can't just leave. Aren't you going to—"

He walked outside.

I jogged after him. "Gunner." The rain whipped around me. "We can't just leave. Gunner, *stop!*"

He whirled around, water running down his face. "Lexi, Bear came after you because you had dirt on him. Now, someone killed him before he got to you. Someone who knew why he was here."

"We can't just leave him here."

He closed the inches between us and grabbed my shoulders. "Lexi, don't you get it? You're next on the list. The Knight Fox did this and he's coming for you, too. The Fox didn't *save* your life from Bear, he wants to take it for himself."

I blinked. I hadn't even considered that the Knight Fox wanted me dead, too.

"And because of that," Gunner continued. "I'm getting

you out of here. Right now. This guy has taken too much from me, from my family, he's not taking you, too." He tossed me over his shoulder.

I gripped onto his back and shifted my weight. "Will you at least call the cops?"

"I'll take care of it." He snapped.

"Sure you will. In some stupid undercover mission that is going to land all of you guys in jail?"

He didn't respond.

My thoughts reeled as my head bobbed with each step. Gunner was going to kill the Knight Fox, there was no question in my mind.

Murder.

Pre-meditated murder.

Capitol one murder.

And if we didn't involve the local police in what we'd just found, I was going to be collateral damage in this rogue mission for revenge.

We breeched the woods and Gunner sat me onto the bike, then slid in front of me.

I wrapped my arms around his waist and buried my head in his back to keep the rain from pelting my face.

The Harley peeled out on the dirt road.

I took a deep breath, inhaling the fresh scent of leather on his back.

I was in deep now.

Too deep.

13

LEXI

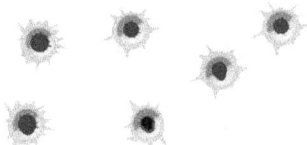

I was soaked to the bone by the time the bike pulled up to Cabin 3. I'm talking sopping wet, hair glued to the side of my face, makeup running down my cheeks, *drenched*.

And *freezing* cold.

I ripped off my helmet.

In addition to cold, wet, and tired, I was emotionally and physically drained and I hadn't eaten a thing since breakfast. It was a monstrous combination for any woman.

I was at my breaking point. I could feel it in my bones.

Gunner took the helmet, along with my hand and helped me off the bike.

And to top it all off, there was Gunner, a guy who seemed to have magical powers over me. A guy who'd just made me an accessory in fleeing a scene of a crime, and his partner in a pending capital murder case.

I didn't know what to think, how to feel. I didn't know how to stop the undeniable pull I felt toward him.

I didn't make bad decisions but ever since laying eyes on

Gunner Steele I'd turned into someone who couldn't form a solid, actionable thought to save my life.

I jogged across the driveway and ducked under the porch. The low base of Gunner's voice carried through the wind. I glanced over my shoulder just as he was clicking off his cell phone.

"Who did you call?"

The rain blurred everything around him as his gaze met mine, his expression stoic and sending a ripple of nerves through my stomach. He ignored my question and slid his phone into his pocket. Yet again, I couldn't read the guy. One minute hot, one minute cold. It was like Gunner Steele was always fighting some epic internal battle.

"Fine," I shook my head and turned around. "Keep your secrets but you're getting soaked."

I began fiddling with the first of what felt like a hundred locks that secured Cabin 3. His arm reached around me, after one thumbprint on an electronic pad that I hadn't even noticed, the locks slid out of place.

I pushed through the front door and kicked off my flip flops. Unsteady hands peeled off my jacket. I was a wreck.

"I need a drink," I muttered, then padded to the kitchen. Because what else was a woman supposed to do after seeing a dead body, fleeing the scene of a murder, and losing all hope of getting her dream job back? I grabbed the whiskey and poured two fingers.

Gunner had made his way into the kitchen, texting feverishly on his phone.

"Something's going on." I handed him the drink, then poured one for myself. "What is it?"

He clicked off the phone and knocked back the double shot like it was water. "I'm having you transferred."

"You're *what?*"

He stared back at me with a neutral gaze. Decision made.

"You're having me transferred? To another cabin? Where?"

"To our office in Colorado."

"*What?* Why?"

"You'll be safer there."

I blinked, my mouth gaping. "You can't just transfer me, Gunner. What am I? A prisoner? Livestock? A cow?"

"I can—and *will*—do whatever is necessary to keep you safe while you're my client."

"Well." My eyebrows shot up along with my defenses. I knocked back my own drink and almost vomited on the floor. Blinking the tears away, I said simply, "No."

"No?"

"No. I'm not going."

His jaw twitched. "I'm not going. I'm staying here." I poured another shot.

"You're going if I have to physically put you into the car myself."

Anger simmered. It was Gunner's way or the highway. Always. "How... what's the plan, then? What plan have you drummed up without even consulting with me?"

He glanced at the clock. "I'm transferring your case to one of our best guards, Madd—"

"*Madd?*"

"At daybreak, Madd will pick you up from here to take you to your new safe place. Only Madd and myself will know its location. He's getting it ready as we speak."

"Then what?"

"Then, as I would have done, Madd will continue to assess your case and either release you when he believes the threat is eliminated, or will discuss your options."

"Like a new identity?"

"That's one of them, yes."

I began pacing. "I don't..." my thoughts whirled as I grabbed the whiskey and downed the shot. This one burned a bit less. I spun around and faced him. "This is bullshit. I'm staying."

"No you're not."

"Yes, I am."

His lips pinched and eyes drifted closed as if biting back a barrage of curses. When his eyes opened again, he said coolly, "It's my job to ensure your safety. My job to put that first. You'll be escorted to Colorado where I have decided you'll be the safest."

"Bullshit."

"So you've said."

"No, I mean bullshit that the only reason you're sending me there is for my *safety*, Gunner." I slammed my hands on my hips and squared off with him. "You don't want me to be involved in what you're planning to do."

"And what, exactly, do you think I'm planning to do?"

"Throw your damn life away." I started pacing again. "You're not calling in Bear's body. If I had to guess, your brothers are already at the scene, which is why I'm not being *transferred* at this exact moment. I'm also guessing you'll get one of the crime lab people that you have in your billionaire pockets to come and assess the scene for evidence. Probably a woman, too, an *attractive* woman that you and your brothers pay *off the books*." *Cool it, Lexi,* was my thought but I kept going, ranting, spiraling out of control. "Then, you'll track down your father's killer and in an ironic twist, you'll spend the rest of your life in jail for doing what you consider is true justice."

His hands curled to fists at his sides.

Yet I freaking kept going. "Do you think your dad would want this? Your brother? Celeste? What about the company you're supposed to be running? What about your brothers?"

And that was it. He exploded.

"I'm doing this *for them!* Don't you see that?" The boom of his voice was like a stun gun that froze me where I stood.

"*Jesus,* Lexi." He strode into the living room and started pacing. "The Knight Fox isn't done. He won't stop until all of us are dead. If I don't end this now, he'll go after the rest of my family. My brothers, Dallas, hell, maybe even everyone who works for us."

The torment in his voice evaporated my anger.

"Gunner..." I crossed the room and put my hand on his arm.

He turned away.

"Look at me."

Nothing.

"Look at me. Please."

Another minute passed before he turned and met my gaze. I'll never forget that moment. The pain, exhaustion, defeat and worry that reflected in the usually steely-eyed *'Good-for-nothing Gunner's'* eyes.

He was broken. Correction—the man was breaking.

"You shouldn't have to sacrifice your own life for theirs. There's got to be another way. There's always another way."

He jerked his arm away and took a few steps back. "You're right, maybe I can call in my super-secret team of chick assassins who I pay *under the table.* Because that's all I'm good for, right? I'm so terrible at business that I can't arrange a single deal that doesn't involve whoring someone out?"

"I'm sorry. I didn't mean it like that."

"Sure you did. Which is exactly my point. I'm not fit to

run a business or take care of my family in any other way than murder or fucking for payment. That's me in a nutshell. Nice to fucking meet you."

"Gunner, I didn't—"

"Since we're being honest here, why did you come here, Lexi? To us? To Steele Shadows? There're a hundred private security firms in the country. Why us?"

I shifted my weight. "Because it was within driving distance of the Dallas airport."

"Bullshit."

"Fine." The rollercoaster of emotions I was on was quickly ramping back up to defensive. "I came to you because I knew you were the best. I'd *heard* you were the best."

"From who?"

"Doesn't matter."

"Look who's keeping secrets now, huh? Fine. Then I want to know something else. Why did you tell Wolf you didn't want me to take your case?"

I'd had no idea Wolf had told him that.

"Answer the question, Lexi. Why the hell do you hate me?"

There are a few things that I didn't handle well. One is being thrown off. The unexpected twist. That was the third that night. One, dead body. Two, being shipped away like a box of cargo. Three, Gunner knowing what I'd said to Wolf. I was done. Officially *done.* I couldn't do it anymore. I couldn't fight another battle. I turned to walk away when a hand gripped my arm, jerking me back.

"Answer the question, Lexi." He snarled in my ear.

I snapped my arm out of his grip and whirled around. "Because you had sex with my sister, Gunner! You one-night-standed my only sister and then dropped her like a bad meal. My sister was worth nothing more than a few hours between the sheets."

Apparently, I wasn't the only one caught off guard. He gaped at me, the wheels spinning so fast in his head that I could almost see them.

The guy didn't remember.

"So, there it is. How does that feel? She calls you *'Good-for-nothing Gunner.'* Do you know that?" The moment the words came out of my mouth I regretted them. But I pushed it aside. I was on a freaking roll and about to dive face-first off the cliff. "You don't remember? You don't remember her, do you? Or is it that you don't care? Well, *I* care, Gunner. Men like you give all men a bad name. *That's* why I didn't want to have anything to do with you."

He blinked. I'd stunned him.

"Sarah York," I continued, because I hadn't needled him enough. "Sarah York, tall, long blonde hair—she bleaches it, by the way—boob job of all boob jobs, basically, every man's dream. That was my sister. She was a bartender at some bar over here for a few weeks before moving on to something else. Before *you* ran her out of town."

His eyes rounded. "Oh my... *God*." He finally spoke. Shaking his head, he stepped over to the window and looked out at the sheets of rain over the mountains. "She worked at Frank's, almost a year ago." He looked over his shoulder, an innocent confusion softening his expression. "She said I *slept* with her?"

I blinked. Uh...

"Oh my God," he repeated, this time with a humorless laugh.

The conversations I'd had with my sister raced through my mind and I realized she'd never specifically said they'd had sex. I'd just assumed.

Oh.... *my*.... *God.*

"I thought—"

"You thought wrong, Lexi. I never touched your sister." He laughed again, this time more manically. "I never *touched* her. The bar was closing up and she asked me to go back to her place. I agreed because I was about five whiskeys in by then. When we got there, she tried to kiss me. I ended it because I didn't want to. And I left." He looked back out the windows. "It was right after my dad died."

I could not *believe* what I was hearing.

His fists curled again, the fifty shades of rage creeping back up. "I cannot *believe* I'm having to justify..." His gaze snapped to mine. He closed the inches between us. "No, Lexi, I didn't have sex with your sister. And you want to know something else? I haven't had sex with anyone in over a fucking year."

I was literally speechless.

"That's right, the middle child of the infamous love-'em-and-leave-'em Steele brothers hasn't had sex in over a year. Shocking isn't it?"

He blew out an exasperated breath, backed up, closed his eyes and held up his hands. "I'm not... I'm not *doing this.*" He turned and stalked to the front door.

"Wait... Gunner..."

"Your car will be here at six a.m.. Nice knowing you, Lexi, even though it's not mutual."

With that, the door slammed, followed by a picture shattering on the floor.

14

GUNNER

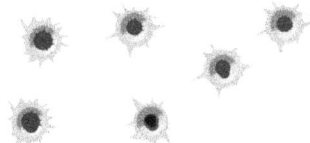

My Harley fishtailed around a corner, the rain mixed with the black night blinding me. I didn't give a shit. If I'm being completely honest here, I was tempting fate. Hell, I was screaming at it.

Faster, faster, faster I sped down the narrow dirt roads, the woods zooming past me in a blurred haze of darkness. My grip tightened on the handlebars, my teeth clenching so hard I was shocked they didn't crack.

Break, you fuckers, go for it.

My heart pounded in an uncontrolled rage, clouding—no, *removing*—all common sense as I went faster and faster in conditions that would have killed most riders already.

Did I want to die?

It wasn't like that was my goal, it was that I didn't care. The most shocking thing of it all was that it wasn't my dad's death, my brother's current state, or Celeste's disappearance that did me in. No, it was a brown-hair, almond-eyed stunner named Lexi York.

What the fuck?

What the *fuck* had just happened?

The woman had cut me deeper than any human on the planet had done before, and let me remind you, I'd met some real winners in my days. I'd been threatened, tortured, beaten in the deepest depths of desert hell. I'd seen it all, felt it all, carried my dad's casket down the aisle, walked in on a hysterical Gage moments after he'd found Feen with a bullet in his head, but after all that, it was a woman named Lexi that threw me over the ledge.

Faster, faster I went, ignoring that little voice in my head telling me to slow down. A bolt of lightning slashed the sky, briefly illuminating the curve ahead that I hadn't realized I'd already come up on. Yeah, I was going too fast.

I tried to slow but not soon enough. I reached the corner going triple what I should have, my tires sliding in a puddle of mud.

That's when everything became a blur.

I remember feeling the bike spin out from under me. My body being propelled into the air. I remember that weightlessness vividly, an out of body experience that reminded me of the stories you hear about someone who'd stared into the white light. There was no white light for me. I remember thinking that was it, that I was going to die—and the *bliss* that came with that thought. I wondered, if it had been caught on camera, if I would have been actually smiling.

Then, I hit the dirt and the world went black.

Sometime later, I woke, my body squeezed between two trees, feeling like I'd just been run over by a tank. I laid there, blinking up at the icy rain pouring down on me, like an extra fuck you from the universe on top of everything else.

Fuck you, indeed.

The worst part—the part that I hate to admit the most—

was that there was a tiny part of me that was disappointed I wasn't dead.

The ultimate mind fuck, huh?

And it was in that moment that I received a kind of clarity I'd never felt before.

I survived that blessed crash for a reason. I was here for a reason. I knew then, without a shadow of a doubt, that it was to avenge my family.

To kill the Knight Fox.

To throw my life away? Abso-fucking-lutely, Lexi York.

With that final thought, I grit my teeth and pushed to a stance, every inch knotted like my limbs had been stretched from end to end. The cell phone that I'd had tucked in my jeans remained intact, shockingly. I did a quick mental scan of myself, taking an extra second to check between my legs, before deciding that nothing was broken. Sprains? Bruised ribs? Maybe a fracture somewhere in there. Not enough to hold me down. If anything, the pain gave me the extra drive I needed to make it back up the ravine I'd tumbled down. As I reached the top, I took a minute to get my bearings realizing I'd gone a lot farther than I realized.

Yeah, I'd been driving way too fast.

I squinted through the trees, zeroing in on the fresh X sliced in one of the trunks. I was a few yards away from the barn Lexi and I had found Bear in not thirty minutes earlier. Lexi might have been right about a few things during her rant, but not that I had already called my brothers and told them about the body. No, I spent the few minutes I had before getting raked over the coals setting up Lexi's extraction from Berry Springs and ensuring her safety.

And wasn't that telling.

My bike was trashed. I grabbed the flashlight and the SIG that had flown from my belt, then picked my way through the underbrush until finally reaching the barn. I stepped inside, and stopped cold.

The chair in the middle of the room was vacant.

Bear was gone. Not a single trace of the man who'd been beaten, tied down, and shot execution style.

Bear was gone—within thirty minutes of me finding him.

The Knight Fox was here, now. I knew it in every inch of my gut.

I shone my light around the windows, the walls, then the floor. Frowning, I kneeled down and peered at the fresh set of muddy boot prints.

My pulse picked up.

I clicked on my cell. Wolf answered on the second ring.

"Wolf, round up the guys and head to Bear's land. To the barn on the east side, about twenty yards past a gate."

"Now?"

"Now."

"Alright, let me—"

"And Wolf, I need something else."

"Yeah?"

"I need you to get me Celeste's shoe size."

15

LEXI

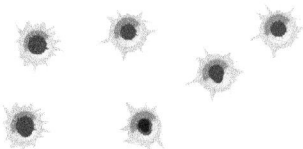

I poured another glass of whiskey, because, well, that seemed like the only thing that could lessen the guilt I was feeling for ripping Gunner to shreds.

What was wrong with me?

I know—I'd officially hit rock bottom, that's what.

I'd lost my job, my freedom, and gotten myself almost killed in the process. I didn't have a car, a cell phone, I couldn't go home. I'd walked into my own nightmare. I was totally lost. The perfect little cherry on top? Seeing the hurt in Gunner's eyes when I'd lashed out at him.

I'd almost chased after him. But at the risk of being some cheesy black and white romance movie, I'd restrained myself. Which was a good thing anyway, because Gunner was down the mountain faster than I could have yelled, *"Stop, my dear!"*

So, whiskey in hand, I paced the cabin until exhaustion gripped me. I finally decided to take off my wet clothes and try to get some sleep until the chariot with my new bodyguard showed up at six a.m.

After mopping up the muddy prints throughout the cabin, I drew myself a bubble bath.

Cure for everything, right?

My stomach was still in knots when I sank into the copper soaking tub. As if built for a woman in need, a small, gold shelf clung to the side, perfect for a book and cocktail.

One for two wasn't bad.

I exhaled and tipped my head back, willing the epic headache that had settled between my temples to go away.

Little did I know, things were about to get worse.

Much worse.

A distant *click* had my eyes shooting open. Call it instinct, call it a sixth sense, but I knew I wasn't alone anymore.

This suspicion was confirmed when a shadow slipped past the bathroom door.

I frantically looked around the bathroom, first, for a towel, second for a weapon. A towel I had, a weapon, I did not. I lifted from the tub, the bubbles oozing over the side as I slipped out.

And that's when it happened.

The lights when out. Blackness engulfed me.

The electricity had been cut.

No vision, no weapon, no options.

Except to fight.

I shifted to the balls of my feet, eyes peeled, trying to make out anything in the inky darkness that surrounded me.

Then, a rush of movement to my side, and we began.

Stars burst in my eyes as a fist connected with my jaw. I caught the next punch, though, and twisted the arm, before sending my knee into my attacker's gut. Then, my feet slipped out from under me—damn the bubbles. I was grabbed from behind and thrown into the vanity. Glass shattered, bottles clambered to the floor. I couldn't get my footing and my attacker knew it. I was tackled into the wall, pain bursting through my head as it bounced off less than an inch from a sharp towel rack. Then, it got real.

Really real.

I was hurled into the tub, water splashing over me as I sank to the bottom.

The icy panic that shot through me was nothing I'd felt before—and that's coming from someone who'd been waterboarded. When the hands wrapped around my neck and shoved me under, I knew that my nine lives had been cashed in. I'd survived one near-drowning incident, the odds of surviving another was nil.

You probably think one would use their arms and legs as weapons while they're being held underwater but the thing is, all you can think about is holding your breath. Your entire focus is to not breathe in. Don't get me wrong, I swiped at the bastard's hands and arms like a feral cat but the grip never wavered.

That's when things got fuzzy.

Have you ever had a dream that someone was chasing you but your legs felt like they were in quicksand? It was kind of like that. My brain was screaming at my arms to move, my legs to kick. Instead, they fell through the water like lead weight.

And then, everything went black.

16

GUNNER

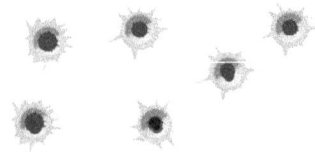

"It's not a full print." Ax shifted the angle of his flashlight.

"Dude, what am I, blind? I know it's not a full print but it's small. Look at the heel, the curve, it's a smaller footprint."

"Every print is smaller than ours, Gunner, what are you, size fourteen?" My brother's gaze followed the footprints to the chair in the middle of the barn. "You're sure it was Sergei Orlov? Bear? Dead in *that* chair, thirty minutes ago?"

"Yep."

"And these prints weren't there then?"

"No. They're fresh, you can tell. Someone removed Bear's body after I found it. Someone was watching me."

I'd informed Ax of every detail other than the fact that Lexi had been with me when we found Bear. Why? Because I knew he'd disapprove. I knew he'd give me a tongue lashing for dragging her into this mess. He'd be right.

"Wolf's measuring a pair of Celeste's shoes now," I said.

"So... what? What're you thinking? *Celeste* is the Knight Fox?"

"All I know is that Celeste is MIA. Wolf hacked into her accounts and she hasn't left town. There's no record of her at the airport, no activity on her cards, nothing. She's still here, Ax. Somewhere."

"The blood in her house indicates she didn't leave on her own accord. Someone took her. Regardless, let's say for a minute you are right, then, there're three scenarios. Celeste either is the Fox, or was with him, or simply walked up on this whole mess."

"She's not wandering the woods in the rain, Ax."

"She's been gone over forty-eight hours. She could be drugged, disoriented. There's no telling. We don't *know*, that's the whole point."

Valid point.

He sat back on his heels and looked me over. His gaze landed on the knot forming under my left eye. "What were you thinking, Gunn?"

"Told you, hit a patch of loose gravel. That's it."

"Bullshit. You're the best rider in the group. You know these roads better than anyone. You were going too fast. Too damn fast like I've told you a hundred times."

"Say it one more time, Axel. I fucking dare you, say it one more time. Trust me, I'd love to break someone's—"

"Jesus *Christ*, Gunner what the hell?"

I surged to my feet as Gage walked into the cabin.

Ax stood. "You need to cool down, dude."

I raised my hands—

"Holy *shiiit!*" Gage's face contorted with disgust as his eyes zeroed-in on my hand. He took a wary step back like he'd walked up on a box of tampons.

Ax followed his gaze. "Whoa, dude. Uh, Gunner, your finger's broken."

I frowned and looked at my left hand where my pinky

finger was, indeed, cracked in half like the number seven. How had that gotten past me?

"Dear *God*, go fix that thing." Gage gagged in the corner.

Ax shook his head. "Dude has literally seen live decapitations in the middle of the desert but can't stomach a broken finger. Anyway, yeah, you might want to take care of that. Having one finger shooting out of the side of your hand may not be great for your love life."

"Actually," Gage's brow cocked with an epiphany of sorts. "If you can twist your hand enough, you might become the most popular bachelor—"

"You're a sick bastard, Gage."

"Hey, it's an erogenous zone, too."

"You learn that in prison?"

"It was an untimely slip of a—"

"*Jesus,* enough. Gage, *enough*." Ax shifted his attention back to me. "Seriously, dude, you look like you got into a fight with a weed-eater..." He flickered a glance to Gage. "Or whatever the hell accidentally slipped into Gage's—"

"Holy hell, I do *not* want to hear the rest of this sentence." Jagg breezed into the barn as casually as he would the grocery store. Just another night at the Steele property.

"What are you doing here?"

"I was down at the range and went up to the main house to see if Dallas had any more of those flax muffin things. Wolf saw me and told me what was up. He's on his way down."

Well, there went the authorities not finding out about Bear's murder.

"Did he get Celeste's shoe size?" I asked.

"Seven and a half according to the pair of flip flops she

had in her office. Side note: Did you know Celeste likes pink? Her whole spare room is decorated in it."

"When did you go in her room?"

"Just now. With Wolf. Have you never been in her room?"

"No." I turned to my brothers. "Have you guys?"

They blinked simultaneously. Not a single one of us had stepped foot into the spare bedroom we'd given to Celeste for nights that she needed to crash on site. Although she rarely used it, she'd apparently taken the time to decorate it. It was another "Celeste surprise." The woman was a secret Martha freaking Stewart.

Jagg kneeled down by the dried blood next to the wooden chair. "I'm assuming you guys haven't informed the local PD of this yet?"

Ax and I exchanged a glance.

"You know I can't let this go, right?" As a state detective, Jagg had his hands in everything and made an effort to stay on the right side of the law. Most of the time, anyway.

"Let us get a few more pictures of the prints and do one more walkthrough, alright?" Ax said patiently.

Well, I wasn't patient. I stepped forward. "Jagg, you're like a brother to me—to us—but you stand in the way of what we're trying to do here, it will be the last time you take a stand."

A second slid by as the former Navy SEAL continued to assess the chair he was examining. Then, he stood and turned to me. "You ever threaten me like that again, Gunner, I'll see to it that those will be the last words that ever come out of your mouth without a dick in it, because at the rate you're going now, you're going to end up in federal prison. Now, get your ass back up to the house and take care of that thing growing out of the side of your hand before I decide to give you a breathalyzer and charge you with DWI and reckless driving."

Ax nodded. "He's right. Go, Gunner. Everything will be here when you get back. Get some food, a drink, take a freaking second man."

I looked back and forth between Ax, Jagg, and Gage. Even Gage was nodding.

Fine, I thought, but food, drink, and resetting my stupid finger was the last thing on my mind. I felt their eyes on me as I stalked out of the barn, and just to be a dick, I took Jagg's truck back up to the house—his fault for leaving the keys in the ignition. After grabbing a handful of guns, ammo, and an ice cold beer, I slid into our covered ATV and took off toward the range.

I stopped at the fork in the trail. To the left, the shooting range, the right, the cabins. I stared at the lights of Cabin 3, twinkling through the rain in the distance.

Lexi.

The woman I would never see again after Madd took her away at six in the morning. Lexi York would no longer be in Cabin 3, she would no longer be in the Knight Fox's sights, no longer be at risk for involving herself in something that could land her in jail. She would no longer be my client.

Mine to watch over, mine to protect.

She would no longer be *mine*.

In an almost involuntary reaction to that thought, my hands jerked the wheel to the right. Although I'd already said my goodbye—punctuated by a slamming door—I just wanted one more look, one last look at the only woman who'd made me question everything. The only woman to make me want to be a better man.

Thunder rumbled through the woods. More rain, more storms coming.

Fitting.

I clicked off the headlights and drove down the trail I knew by heart wondering what Lexi was doing, what she was thinking.

If she was thinking about me.

The trail dipped and when I peaked—blackness.

It was as if the entire world had gone dark.

I looked over my shoulder at the main house still lit up in the distance, then back toward cabin 3 where all the lights were suddenly off.

Not even the outdoor security lights that stayed on twenty-four seven. Not even the porch lights.

The hair on the back of my neck prickled.

Something was wrong.

Something was very wrong.

I skidded to a stop behind the cabin, pulled my gun and slid out of the ATV. A dark silhouette in the bathroom caught my eye.

Then, a body flying through the air.

"Lexi!" Her name screamed from my lips as I sprinted up the yard. The front door was locked. My thumbprint didn't work which told me the electricity had been cut, so I took a few steps back and blasted through the three deadbolts. I barreled through the living room and into the bathroom where Lexi's limp body lay submerged underwater.

~

Lexi

. . .

I woke up to blackness, with Gunner's mouth over mine, his fists pounding into my chest. Coughing, spurting, I was rolled onto my side until the spinning and gagging stopped.

I was soaked. My hair, my skin, the floor underneath me slick with water and bubbles.

I was confused, nauseous, my brain a jumbled fog trying to figure out what had just happened. Fear bubbled up in the form of panic and tears.

A hand stroked my back.

I blinked up at the silhouette kneeled over me on the floor.

"Gunner?" The weakness of my voice had my focus centralizing. I didn't recognize the voice coming out of me. It was like a little girl. A terrified, little girl.

"I'm right here." In contrast to mine, his voice was low and deep, a calming timbre that anchored me.

Gunner was there. I was okay.

A flash of lightning illuminated the tense lines of his face, the laser focus on me.

He leaned down, wrapped his arms around me and slowly lifted me to a seated position. I was stark-raving naked but I didn't care. Probably the first time in my life that I didn't care. The room spun around me. I buried myself in his chest.

And let the tears fall.

It was like a dam breaking. Every emotion was releasing into a hyperventilating, snot-sucking, bawling-my-eyes-out mess.

My protector, my anchor, held me through it, rocking back and forth on the cold, wet, bathroom floor.

Eventually, I pulled back and without thinking, wiped my nose on his forearm. Classy.

He pulled down a towel from the rack and draped it over

my shoulders.

"Thank you."

"You're welcome."

I gripped the soft, cotton towel tighter around me, the realization of exactly *how* naked I was, and how dressed *he* was, making me feel more vulnerable than I already did.

"Come on, let's get you off this floor."

I was swept into Gunner's arms and carried into the living room, still dark with no electricity. I was placed gently in the leather arm chair, where he wrapped a thick flannel blanket around me.

No words were spoken as he turned to the fireplace. I watched him methodically stack logs and kindling with the speed and skill of someone who'd done it a million times. Minutes later, the fire was roaring, the red hot glow of the flames dancing on the walls around us.

He kneeled at my feet. For a moment, we said nothing at all, simply stared at each other.

No words needed to be spoken.

He reached forward and tucked a strand of hair behind my ear.

"I need to make a few calls."

I nodded.

"I'll be right back."

I watched as Gunner pulled the cell phone from his pocket and stepped into the bedroom.

The man that held my safety in the palm of his hand.

The man who had just saved my life.

"Gunner?" I sat up, the desperation cracking my voice as I called out after him.

He was by my side in an instant.

I grabbed his hand. "... Don't leave me."

"I wasn't planning on it."

17

LEXI

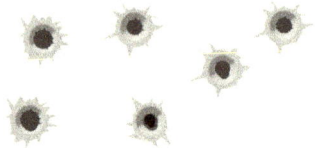

Ten minutes later, Gunner had made his calls and completed a perimeter check outside. He stepped through the back door, the roaring fire illuminating the alert focus on his face. It was the first time I noticed the cuts along his cheeks, the black eye, the mud and grass stains all over his clothes.

"Gunner." I shot up in my seat, gripping the blanket around my chest. "What *happened*? Are you okay?"

He blinked, as if taking a second to register what I was talking about. "Oh. Took a tumble off the bike."

I scanned his body and the horrified gasp that came out of me sounded more like a gargle. If I hadn't thrown up everything in my stomach already, I would have vomited right there in the chair.

He followed my gaze to his pinky finger, bent like the number seven. "Oh. Yeah... I was supposed to fix this... Be right back."

Gunner disappeared into the bedroom. After a faint groan, he walked out with a fresh sheen of sweat on his brow. He raised his hand, the finger back in place. "Good as new."

"Did you just *break* it back into place?"

"How else was I supposed to fix it?"

I shook my head. Of course he fixed his own broken bones, because who didn't?

"How are you feeling?" He crossed the room, flexing his newly reformed hand.

"Good. I promise. Gunner," I reached out from the blanket and squeezed his other hand. "You saved my life."

His jaw twitched and I knew what he was thinking. He should have gotten there sooner. A guy like Gunner blamed himself for everything. He dropped my hand, took a step back and changed the subject.

"I can't get the electricity back on. The generator's out, too. We won't have power the rest of the evening."

The rain had picked up, a heavy buzz on the roof.

"What about the main house? Can we go there?"

"No." He shook his head. "No. Too many access points, too many people. The smaller the area, the easier to contain."

"But your brothers are in the main house. Isn't that safer? Safety in numbers, right?"

He looked away.

I cocked my head. "You think the Knight Fox could be someone from the inside. From your family or company. Don't you?"

After a moment, he heaved out a breath and began pacing. "Your door was locked from the inside, Lexi. Someone either knew, or bypassed the security code, let themselves in, then locked it back from the inside. The electricity lines and generator are intact, which makes me think there was some sort of system override."

My eyes rounded. "Who would have access to your security?"

"Everyone here at the house. I've already left a voicemail with Wolf."

The thought was nothing short of horrifying. Fort Knox had been infiltrated. Everyone, including me, was now at risk.

I chewed my lower lip. "Did you see him? My attacker?"

"No, I had to blow the locks to get in, which tipped him off. Whoever it was jumped out the bathroom window and took off."

"*Jumped* out the bathroom window?"

He nodded.

"That's got to be twenty feet down."

"Seventeen and a half."

"Well considering they're not lying on the ground with broken bones, I'm assuming it's someone who knew what they were doing."

"Did you get a good look?"

"No." I shook my head. "Not even a glimpse. When the electricity was cut, it went pitch black..." I swallowed the knot in my throat. "It happened so fast. I... I—"

"Hey." Gunner stepped to the edge of my chair, an uncomfortable expression crossing his face. He searched the room as if looking for something. "Hey, let's..." He landed on the kitchen. "Eat. Let's eat."

A laugh spurted out of me. "Eat?"

"Well, we're here, aren't we? And you need to eat." His lopsided smile told me this was his desperate attempt to calm me, to distract me from what had happened. To ease me. He didn't like seeing me scared. Little did he know, his presence was enough to make me feel secure.

I smiled. "Okay, well, I'm supposed to cook dinner for us remember? I lost the bet."

"No." He put his hand on my shoulder as I tried to rise. "No, sit. Please. You need to... ... dammit, just *sit,* Lexi."

A softer side of Gunner beginning to show through. Despite his best effort to conceal it.

After a gentle squeeze of my shoulder, he disappeared into the kitchen. Thirty seconds later, I was handed a glass of wine over my shoulder. Five minutes after that, an ornate wooden tray was placed on my lap. His, on the coffee table next to the fire, followed by a fifth of whiskey. No glass.

I looked down at the spread on my lap. Slices of fresh turkey, ham, three different kinds of cheeses, olives, grapes and sliced strawberries, all thoughtfully decorated on the plate. To the side, an overflowing bowl of Cheetos—the crunchy kind, not the puffs.

"Sorry, no microwave."

I smirked. "Funny that's the first appliance that comes to mind when you think about cooking. There's something called an oven and a stove you know."

"I keep spare boxes of bullets in the oven."

"A ticking time bomb. Nice work."

A smile tugged the corner of his lips, then a subtle line of concern crossed his forehead. "Is it okay, though? I can arrange something else... I can have the guys bring us something different if—"

"No. No, it's perfect, actually. Light, healthy, with a side of Cheetos and wine. Pretty much my ideal Friday night."

He glanced down.

"I'm not joking."

"Well, bon appetit, then."

He popped a slice of ham into his mouth. I did the same. Despite the fact I'd almost died an hour earlier, I was ravenous. We ate in a comfortable silence, with Gunner checking his phone every few seconds and taking swigs of whiskey in between.

I watched him, the quick, mechanical way he ate, as if only fueling his body for the next fight. His eyes were sharp, every so often scanning the windows, the doors, shifting to me for a split-second before focusing back on his food.

"Do you ever relax?" I asked.

This seemed to catch him by surprise. He looked up, blinked, then said, "There are things to be done, so they get done." It was such a simple—calculated—answer that left no room for a response. Gunner was a pro at avoiding any conversation that went beyond surface level. Hell, the guy was a pro at avoiding ninety-percent of conversations.

And I was up for that challenge.

I popped a strawberry in my mouth and sipped my wine. "Okay, let's play a game while we eat."

His brow cocked.

"You don't play games?"

"No."

This guy.

"We'll start easy, then. What's your favorite food?"

"Bacon."

"Just bacon?"

"BLTs. Or anything with bacon. Pork pretty much sums it up."

I grinned because what else did I expect?

"Caramelized sodium. Got it. Favorite movie?"

"Charlotte's Web."

"Oh, you're being funny? Did Gunner Steele just crack a joke?"

"Not a joke. My brothers and I must've watched it a hundred times growing up."

"While eating BLTs?"

"While target shooting."

"Jerk."

His head tilted. "How's that piece of ham you just popped in your mouth?"

I frowned.

He grinned. Pleased with himself, he continued, "Dirty Harry is my all-time favorite movie."

"A movie about hunting vicious psychopaths. Hmm, target shooting, hunting... I'm seeing a theme here."

"Made a whole career out of it."

"And the world is better because of it. I mean that."

His gaze flickered to me, then back to his food.

"Okay, next, what's—"

"Oh, hell no. I'm not the only one playing this little game. You have to answer, too."

"Okay, fine. My favorite movie is... Notorious."

He wrinkled his nose in horrified disbelief. "The movie about that rapper? 2 Pac, or Biggie, Smallie... or whatever their names were?"

Laughter barreled out of me. "No, not that one. And that takes care of me asking what kind of music you *don't* like."

"If you're going to talk, talk. You know? I don't get it."

I laughed again. "Agreed. Anyway, no, not that Notorious."

His brows arched. "You're not talking about the iconic 1946 spy flick produced by Alfred Hitchcock starring Cary Grant and Ingrid Bergman? Are you?"

"You know it?"

"Yeah, I know it." A fleeting moment of happiness sparkled in his eye. "I watched it with my dad a few times. I'm surprised *you* know it."

"Because you assumed my favorite movie is Legally Blonde?"

"Naw, for you, I'd go with The Notebook."

"Never saw it."

"You're shitting me."

"Gross. No I'm not *shitting* you. You've seen it?"

"Hell, no. I just thought every human with a pair of breasts had seen it. Ten times each."

I glanced down at my barely-B-cups. "That takes care of me, then."

"Now you're the one being funny."

I blushed. "No Notebook. Not really into tear-jerking chick flicks."

He studied me in that ever-assessing way that seemed innate to Steele brothers. "Hang on. Back to these boobs..."

"Not every woman is blessed with double-D's, you know."

"One, life isn't a Motley Crew video—trust me—and two, not every man wants them."

I looked down and shifted under his gaze that was reading my insecurities like a book.

Finally, he said, "Okay. Back to the movies... So, really, Notorious, huh?"

"It's true. I've seen it countless times. One might say it's the entire reason I wanted to become an undercover agent."

"Or, a prequel to your expose."

"Kicking me when I'm down. Classic."

He winked, relaxing. "It's a great film. Back in the days where men smoked cigars and drank brandy all day while women waited at home, preparing that four course meal you promised me."

"You're an ape." I rolled my eyes. "Okay, we know you don't like rap. What's your favorite music?"

"What do you think my favorite music is?"

"Heavy metal."

"Because I'm a raging jarhead asshole?"

"I didn't call you a jarhead." I winked.

"It's classic country. Merle Haggard, Willie Nelson. Good ol' country. Not that pop crossover crap these kids listen to these days."

"Spoken like a true cowboy. Dirty Harry, cigars, male chauvinism, and Merle Haggard. I'm starting to understand why there's no Missus."

"You forgot the brandy." He grinned. "What do you listen to? Pussy Riot?"

"You just said that so you could say that word."

"It's incredible how many conversations it can be worked into."

"I bet. No Pussy Riot for me. I like—"

"I'm sorry, I'm going to need you to repeat—"

"Pervert."

He winked, again.

"I like the blues."

"Stevie Ray?"

"Best guitarist of all time if you ask me."

He leaned forward on his elbows, a new kind of spark in his eyes. Heat.

"Favorite pastime?" I asked.

"Eating whatever you're cooking in six-inch heels."

"You've really clung onto this haven't you?"

He skimmed the blanket that covered my naked body. "Hard not to."

My cheeks flushed for the second time.

I looked around the small, one bedroom cabin. The rain pounding the windows outside, the flames from the fire flickering along the walls. Talk about a romantic movie.

Butterflies tickled my stomach. Gunner was going to be staying the night there, with me.

Just us two.

Alone.

My gaze shifted to his, my head almost jerking back at the intensity of his gaze—as if he was thinking the exact same thing.

Shit, was all I could think.

Nerves now fluttering inside me, I took a hefty sip of my wine.

"Are men and women equal?"

"Yes." His response both immediate and surprising. "And why do I feel like this isn't a game anymore?"

"What do you find most attractive in a girl?"

"Perseverance. A close second? Your naked body, under that blanket."

My grip tightened around my wineglass.

He continued, "I like a woman who goes after what she wants. Sticks with it. Sticks with it through the hard times."

It was a thinly veiled—very loaded—statement.

Message received.

He took a sip of whiskey. "What's the most attractive thing in a guy to you?"

"Confidence." Then, I don't know if it was the wine or the way he was looking at me but I said, "Next question. Favorite sexual position?"

"All of them."

I felt the heat spread between my legs and decided that unless I was going to throw myself on this guy at that very moment, I needed to change the subject. I settled back into the chair and took a silent deep breath. We shifted our attention to the flames flicking, the sexual tension in the room hotter than the raging fire.

"If you could live anywhere in the world, where would it be?"

His face hardened. He stared into the fire a second before saying, "Anywhere but here."

It was a real, honest, and so sad answer.

"I'm sorry about your brother."

He grabbed the whiskey, chugged, then set it down with a quick nod.

"He's the oldest, right?"

"Right. Just over a year older than me."

"And Gage and Axel are younger, right?"

"Two years, yes."

I sipped my wine, watching him over the rim. I felt like he was finally starting to open up. *Allowing* himself too. I wanted to know everything that was Gunner Steele, why he was the way he was, why he thought the way he did, why he wore such a thick coat of armor.

I wanted to know more about the man I only saw glimpses of. The man with a heart, a softness, a desire to please, to be more than he was. A desire to make others happy.

"Why didn't you sleep with my sister?"

His brows raised with a flash of surprise. He slid his elbows onto his knees and considered his answer.

"She wasn't for me."

"I call bullshit."

"I think we've already established gambling is not in your favor."

"Seriously, Gunner, don't deflect. Why? Why didn't you sleep with her? I want to know. Sarah is *everyone's* type. Trust me on this."

He studied me for a moment. "She stole one of your boyfriends, didn't she?"

Now it was my turn to be surprised. "How the hell..."

"I'm good at reading people."

I shouldn't have been surprised. The guy built a career on reading situations and adapting to them. One wrong decision, one wrong read, could cost lives.

"Well, at the risk of sounding like a walking cliché, you're right. We were seventeen. Sarah was always the popular one—tends to happen when you have D cups by high school."

"There's those D's again."

"*Anyway*, my boyfriend of six months—which was a long time in high school years—decided to take a spin with the 'popular York sister,' and she let him." I took a sip of wine. "And you want to know the sick part? I think that was his plan all along. I think he only used me to get to her. I wasn't the star York, ever."

"I know the feeling."

"Do you? Because I'm pretty sure you could have any woman on the planet."

He glanced away. At least he didn't try to deny it.

"You seriously haven't had sex in a year?"

"Hard to believe, Lexi?"

"Yes. It is."

"I'm a lot of things but a liar isn't one of them."

"When was your last girlfriend?"

"Can't remember."

"You can't remember when your last committed relationship was?"

He shrugged.

I laughed. "Typical billionaire playboy."

"Now that's a cliché."

I sat back. "But you're different. You're embarrassed."

"Of what?"

"Of how much money you have."

He mindlessly picked at his grapes. "I'd give it all away, Lexi. Every single penny."

"Why? Why do you say that? Do you know how many people would kill to have a fraction of what you have?"

"It's not me." He blew out a breath. "The houses, the cars, the things. The business. It's not *me*. A billionaire playboy, I am not." He cocked his head. "You always this quick to judge someone?"

"Well, if you'd open up more, I wouldn't have to. I just go with the outside-looking-in obvious—"

"Obvious? So it must be obvious then that the reason I haven't committed to a woman is because when I joined the military, I chose a life where I was gone over three hundred days a year. A life where every day could be my last. A kind of life that I wasn't going to put a family through. A woman deserves more than a husband who's never home, and when he is, is only thinking of the next fight. Yeah, I've slept with a lot of women, Lexi, but I made sure they knew up front that was all it was. And guess what? They *never cared*. How's that for a mind fuck? How's that for making you feel like you're worth nothing more than a quick lay? Between my dad, Phoenix, this new damn life I'm living, and shallow women, yeah, I made the decision to quit having sex. I've messed around with a few girls, sure. I am a man after all, but no sex. Not until it means something. My brothers would laugh me out of the house if they knew but it was a decision I'd made. So, tell me Lexi, was all that obvious?"

I was speechless.

He leaned forward, pinned me with a gaze that confirmed I'd struck a chord. "I'm betting that much wasn't obvious, was it, Lexi?"

"I'm sorry."

"It wasn't obvious was it?"

"No. No, it wasn't." I leaned forward. "Gunner, you can't carry all this weight.... Seriously, Gunner. Life is too short, trust me, I—"

He surged to his feet, his strawberries tumbling to the floor. "You think I don't know that, Lexi? You think I don't know life is too fucking short? My brother is hanging onto life by a thread in the ICU right now, my dad is six feet in the ground. And *you*, you, almost..." He jabbed his fingers through his hair. *"Dammit.* ... I know all about life being too short, Lexi." He began stalking back and forth.

I set my wine on the table, stood, and in only my blanket, walked over to him. He turned his back.

I moved behind him and tipped my forehead into his back.

A heavy minute passed.

"I'm sorry," he mumbled.

"No. No, Gunner don't be." I put my hand on his arm and turned him to me. "Sit."

He didn't budge.

"Sit." I pulled him to the couch. After forcing him to sit, I kneeled in front of him, the blanket pluming around my body.

"Talk to me."

His gaze finally met mine, the fight gone from those bloodshot indigo eyes.

"Talk. Talk to me, Gunner. Start with what happened tonight. I've been on the back of a motorcycle with you. You didn't just get in an *accident.* Tell me why you were so reckless."

His silence was infuriating. I would have given my soul for him to open up fully to me. Hell, to *anyone.*

Clenching my teeth, I grabbed the whiskey, tipped it up

and chugged enough to prove I could, then shoved it in his face. He swigged, then passed it back.

"Now. Talk Gunner."

"You want me to talk, Lexi? Want to hear how screwed up I really am? Fine. When Dad died, everything got flipped on its head. My brothers and I quit the military and moved home. Phoenix took his place as the oldest brother, and all the responsibility that comes with that, while the rest of us struggled to find our way. Gage found his in every woman's tits within the tristate area, and Ax found his in books and climbing damn trees, or whatever that guy does in the woods. Me? I can't count how many bullets I've shot in the range. If I'm not there, I'm in the garage, working on my cars. The thing is—the irony of it all is—that now everything has fallen in my lap. *My* lap. I'm next in line, so it's me, the screwed-up rebellious Steele brother. The family business, all the money, taking care of my brothers, everything is on me, the guy worst suited to handle that kind of stuff."

Tears swam in his eyes and I literally held my breath hoping he wouldn't close up again.

"It should have been me, Lexi. I should be the one lying in ICU right now. Feen didn't deserve this, I did."

I gripped his leg. "Don't say that, Gunner," I kissed his knee through his jeans, still wet from the rain. "Don't say that."

He sniffed and steeled himself. The single tear was gone as quickly as it came.

"Why does it all have to be on your shoulders?" I asked. "I don't get it. Can't your brothers help? You're shouldering too much."

"Someone has to take the seat at the head of the table. It's how it works. It's how our family works. Someone leads the pack." He fisted his hands on his knees. "My whole life, no one has ever had faith in me. No one has ever expected anything from me. And now? Yeah, *now* they have expectations. They expect me to screw up. To send decades of my father's work into the ground."

"I have faith in you, Gunner."

His gaze met mine.

"I have faith in you that you're going to succeed. That you're going to come out of this. You're strong enough to. That you're not going to throw your life away to get revenge for your family." I gripped his knee, tears welling. "Please don't kill anyone Gunner, please. Gunner, I have faith in you."

I looked down at his feet, trying to blink the tears away. A minute slid by. I could feel his eyes boring into me.

"You want to know why I didn't sleep with your sister, Lexi?" He lightly grabbed my chin, tipped my face to him. He leaned down, inches from my lips. My breath stopped. "She wasn't for me. She wasn't the one."

His hand slid over mine.

"She wasn't the one to crack my fucking heart open."

18

GUNNER

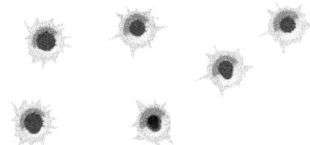

The moment the words came out of my mouth I froze. I'm talking deer in headlights, froze.

I pulled away from her as a bear would recoil from a trap.

What. The. *Fuck?*

It was like an uncontrollable vomit of emotions was barreling out of me.

Was it the whiskey?

Was it her?

It didn't matter. All that mattered was that this woman had just singlehandedly turned me into a dickless pussy that couldn't control a single word out of his mouth. I didn't open up. To anyone. A defense mechanism, whatever, but I'd always found that life was a lot easier without baring my fucked up soul to anyone. No one understood. No one got me.

No one cared to get me.

Except Lexi York.

It was exactly what I didn't need at that time of my life.

Emotions made you messy, weak. Had a way of clouding even the most levelheaded men. Believe me, I'd seen it.

So what did I do then? The only thing I could think to do.

Abort, abort, abort.

I cleared my throat, grabbed her plate, mine, then pushed to a stance and practically jogged out of the damn room.

After dropping the plates in the sink, I gripped the counter, bowed my head and blew out a breath.

"I'm sorry."

My head jerked up and I turned to the woman standing in the doorway, the flames from the fire at her back silhouetting her long, silky neck and bare shoulders, a milky white that reminded me of warm, creamy vanilla.

"No." I shook my head. "No, don't say that."

"I shouldn't have pressed. I'm sorry, I'm sorry, I just—"

"Don't you get it, Lexi? You can't continue this journey with me. I'm not going to promise what you want me to. You can't be involved in it. I've taken people down with me in my past. I'm not going to do it again. You're too good for this. You're too good for me, Lexi. Don't you see that?"

"Gunner," she said in a breathless plea. "You won't do it. You won't kill the Knight Fox—"

"I have to, Lexi!" I exploded.

She stepped back, the fear in her eyes ripping my heart out.

I closed my eyes, exhaling. "Go." I dismissed her with a wave of my hand. "Go to bed."

She didn't move.

"Get out of here, Lexi."

My fists clenched at my side and I had to literally restrain myself from punching the wall next to me.

"Go."

~

Lexi

I blinked, a tear sliding down my cheek.

It was like watching someone spiral out of control. Nothing I could do or say would change his mind. I knew that now. He was walking death. The saddest part was that he wouldn't have it any other way.

He couldn't even look at me, it was like he couldn't even stand to be in my presence. You know the most screwed up part of it? I still wanted to help him.

But as I looked at Gunner, the vein pulsating in his neck, the fists at his sides, I knew nothing was going to get through to him.

He'd made up his mind.

And that was that.

So, I turned and disappeared into the bedroom with the only light pooling at the doorway from the fire in the living room.

The air was heavy, still, silent, except for the crackling logs. I sat on the edge of the bed and stared at the doorway.

Although I might have cracked open Gunner Steele's heart, it was temporary.

I was a fool to think there was any way to break through that shell. I was a fool to have feelings for Gunner Steele.

A knot formed in my throat.

I knew sleep would evade me, so I sat, still, and said a prayer for the man in the kitchen.

. . .

Seconds ticked to minutes, minutes to an hour as I listened to the fire burning from the living room. I knew Gunner hadn't left. I knew he wouldn't leave me.

Sometime around midnight, I tiptoed to the doorway.

This time, it was my heart that cracked open.

Motionless, Gunner sat on the edge of the couch, his head in his hands and an empty beer at his side.

A broken man.

A shattered man.

A completely lost man.

I crossed the room to his side.

His head didn't raise, his body didn't move.

"Hey," I whispered.

Nothing.

I placed my hand on his shoulder. "Hey."

Another moment passed before he looked up, his eyes shaded, puffy, red-rimmed.

He'd been crying.

Gunner Steele was human.

The vulnerability in his face ruined me.

His hand reached for me. Tears filled my eyes as he guided me between his legs, wrapped his hands around my waist and buried his head into my stomach. Blinking the tears away, I stroked his hair.

And let him cry.

The fire roared in front of us, reflecting the intensity of a moment I knew I'd remember for the rest of my life. Gunner, with his pride obliterated, his armor shattered. His heart right there on the floor.

His grip tightened around me.

"I'm sorry," he whispered.

A tear fell from my cheek.

"It's okay," I whispered back. "It's okay."

His face lifted, tears sliding down his face as his hand slid under the blanket. His fingertips blazed a trail of shockwaves over my bare hips.

He slowly unwrapped the blanket in an erotic removal of my own armor. My own shield. Goosebumps rippled over my skin as the flannel fell to the floor.

I stood naked in front of him, the heat of the fire at my back, the heat of his gaze even hotter.

His large, calloused hands ran down my sides waving like an hourglass with my curves, stopping on my ass.

He leaned in, kissed my stomach, my belly button, then yanked me to him with a sense of desperation, an urgency, that had my heart skipping. His lips, his breath against my hips had warmth funneling below, my insides turning to water. My body was already screaming out for him.

He pulled me onto his lap.

"I'm sorry," he whispered again. "I should have never spoken to you like that. I'm sorry, Lexi."

"Gunner," I rested my hands on his shoulders. "Shhh..."

He looked up at me. His hand slid through my hair to the back of my head, sending tingles over my scalp as he searched my face. Then, after one last piercing gaze, he pulled my face to his and kissed me. Soft, slowly at first, with a passion that sent my head spinning and fireworks exploding in my head. Deep, powerful, demanding. Unrestrained, with the release of someone who was finally letting go, and I was the lucky girl on the receiving end of all that pent up emotion. His hands dropped to my body, stroking my bare skin, my arms, my sides, my breasts, my nipples prickling at this touch.

I was lost in him, in his kiss, in his touch.

In the *fire* that was Gunner Steele.

We dropped to the floor together, the passion between

us too much for the small couch. The coffee table was kicked to the side, whiskey tumbled to the ground. I lowered to my back, pulling him with me.

"No." He muttered between kisses. "No."

"What?"

He lifted me from the floor as if I were ten pounds and cradled me in his arms.

"A woman like you is too good for the floor."

I fell in love. That was the moment I fell in love.

Like a new bride, I was carried into the bedroom and laid softly on the bed. I watched as Gunner lit one, two, three long-stemmed candles, the glow dancing along the walls.

He turned, his gaze locking on mine.

"Do you want this, Lexi?"

"More than anything."

"There's no going back."

No, I already knew there was no going back. There was never going back after one taste of Gunner Steele. I slid off the bed, desperate for him not to change his mind. My hands began working his belt. My lips met his.

He pulled off his shirt and kicked out of his boots. The heat radiated off his shredded body covered not only in tattoos, but scars as well. Yes, the layers and layers of Gunner Steele kept unpeeling.

His pants hit the floor, the long, thickness of his erection springing against my stomach.

It took everything I had not to take a peek. I was lifted into the air, my legs wrapping around his waist, his rock-hard cock cradling my ass. Kissing, kissing, kissing we collapsed on the bed.

Lightning flashed outside, thunder boomed in the distance.

His lips traveled down my stomach igniting my skin with each inch. The throbbing between my legs like a pulsating prickle as he reached the crease of my hips.

Oh *God,* was all I could think.

Little did I know what he had in mind.

He widened my legs, gripped my ankles and pressed them up and forward, exposing me to him in the most intimate way. The cool air swept over my heated skin, as if I needed a reminder exactly how exposed I was.

My stomach danced with nerves. I squeezed my eyes shut with a giddy mixture of excitement and embarrassment. My hand found the top of his head as his lips ran along my inner hips. The tickle had me jumping, the jerk had his grip tightening and telling me I wasn't going anywhere.

I willed my insecurities aside and focused on the eagerness of his tongue, teasing me.

"You're the most beautiful woman I've ever seen in my life, Lexi York."

Then, his mouth closed over me, the slickness sliding over my throbbing, sensitive skin, the heat sending a firestorm through my system as he dined on me like it was his last dinner. Shiver after shiver my body responded in a way I'd never felt before. I writhed under him, fisting the comforter in my hands, feeling like I was about to explode in a million beautiful little pieces. I dipped my chin back and moaned, the heat turning to tingles as he lapped me up.

If I thought it couldn't get better, I was sorely mistaken.

His tongue slid over my clit, followed by a light flick, then a soft suckle that sent me spiraling.

"Oh my God, Gunner," I whispered, the words coming out in a breathless plea. "Gunner."

My desperation was met with increased pressure against

the tiny, swollen bud. Swirling, his tongue played, captivated my body, stealing all sense of self-control. I wanted one thing, only one thing—for him to be inside me. To *feel* him. For that intensity to fill me up.

But he wasn't ready.

He sucked harder, faster, until the orgasm finally ripped through me. I floated through the air in a weightless euphoria, wave after wave, until finally, I landed.

My eyes opened to Gunner hovering over me, watching me orgasm with a fire in his eyes that sent a shot of adrenaline through my languid body. You'd think after an orgasm like that, I couldn't move, that I'd be spent. But it was the opposite.

The total opposite.

An animalistic desire took over me.

I grabbed his neck, pulled him down onto me and crushed my lips onto his.

"Have sex with me," I growled in his ear. "I want you inside me, now, Gunner. *Now.*" I begged.

He pulled away and cupped my face in his hands.

His eyes bored into my soul. "You're the one, Lexi," he whispered. "You're the one."

The words hit me like a Mack truck.

His tip found my opening. My breath caught, knowing that moment was going to change our lives forever. Staring back at him, I knew he felt the same. And with that unspoken promise, he slid into me.

My eyes squeezed shut at the power, the girth of him. Jaw clenching, I stretched around him—for him—the pain punctuating the power that was Gunner Steele. A man of all men. A moan escaped my lips as he pushed deeper, my body softening and wetting as he filled me to places I'd never been.

"You okay?"

"Yes. Gunner. Yes." I dug my nails into his back, thrusting my hips forward.

"Mmm," his moan faded with the slow rhythm we'd established.

I breathed into his neck, squeezing myself around him, wanting to experience every sensation he was giving me. I couldn't get enough.

"Shit, Lexi."

His breathing picked up along with his pace, each push hitting deeper and deeper inside me. On the brink of exploding again, he grabbed my waist, flipped me over, and rolled me on top of him, lifting me just above his tip. His muscles flexed as he stared up at me.

"I want to see you. Your beautiful body. I want to watch you come again."

He slowly lowered me onto his erection, my entire body tensing from head to toe. I was breathless. Completely breathless. I moaned as my hair cascaded down my breasts, even that delicate touch heightening my senses. I searched for anything to grip, to help anchor the size of him. He grabbed my hands. The sensation was so intense I had to take a minute to adjust, for my body to accept him.

Slowly, testing, I rounded my hips, my clit grinding against his springy pad of hair. My body relaxed around him inciting an entirely new sensation. Biting my lip, I closed my eyes, and began the ride.

His hands massaged my thighs as I began to slowly rock back and forth.

"That's it, baby. Take it. Take it all. That's it..."

His hands drifted to my breasts, squeezing my nipples as my clit rubbed against him with each dip of my hips. And then, everything started again. The warmth, the tingling, the waves of shivers through my body.

"Oh, fuck, Lexi." His large, strong hands gripped my waist, lifting me with each thrust as I rode him. Faster, faster, gasping for breaths, my body lifted up and down. My fingers dug into his chest, my brain spinning.

Our eyes locked.

Mine filled with tears.

Words unspoken, souls seen, we shattered together.

19

GUNNER

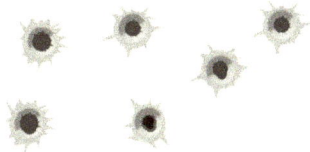

An hour had passed as I watched Lexi sleeping in my arms, the steady rise and fall of her chest against mine, the way her brown hair fanned over the pillow. I watched her breathe, matching her rhythm, feeling a peace, a calmness I can honestly say I'd never felt before. She was like a human muscle relaxer, easing the tornado swirling inside me, taking my hand and welcoming me into the closest thing to heaven I could imagine. There was no stress, no thinking, only *that* moment. Between us. For the first time in my life, I felt a stillness, a quietness, in my body.

In my soul.

Peace.

Lexi York was beautiful, stunning, perfect.

Mine.

Mine, mine, *mine*.

Except that she wasn't. She couldn't be. My dream woman was being shipped off to Colorado in less than five hours and I was as good as a walking dead man, sure to spend the rest of my days in prison. It wouldn't work. It couldn't work.

She'd wanted me to promise her something that I couldn't.

As quickly as it came, the peace lifted and an overwhelming wave of sadness washed over me. Then, for a second—*a split second*—I questioned everything. Maybe she was worth it. Maybe *we* were worth it. Maybe she and I could escape together. Leave everything. Maybe we could make it work.

Maybe I wouldn't pull that trigger.

Maybe I loved this woman.

Which was exactly why I had to let her go.

It was so fucked up.

Such was my life.

As if on cue, my cell vibrated from the living room. Careful not to wake her, I slipped out of bed—out of the warmth, the softness, the tranquility that I'd found, if only for a few hours.

I padded to the living room where the fire was just beginning to die down.

The illuminated screen was like a beacon through the darkness. Something inside me shifted to alert. I clicked on the phone and my stomach dropped to my feet. The culmination of the last year, the last hours I'd just had with Lexi, hell, my whole life, had exploded with one text—

Wolf: *I've found the Knight Fox.*

My heart kicked-started like an overdose. I typed a response.

Where is he?

. . .

Wolf: *The cell phone associated with the shell company was just turned on. Just south of our property.*

Where, exactly?

Wolf: *Can't pin the exact location. I know there's an old hunting cabin around there. Told you first. What do you want to do?*

What did I want to do? My daze shifted to the bedroom where Lexi slept. Where she'd asked me to promise I wouldn't kill the Knight Fox.

Wolf: *Gunner? Need to know...*

Have Gage and Ax meet me at the range in 5. Don't tell anyone else.

Wolf: *You got it. See you in 5.*

I closed the text and opened another.

Dallas: *Hey. Everything okay?*

. . .

Where are you?

Dallas: *The main house. What's wrong?*

Nothing. I've got to take care of something and I'm hoping you can keep an eye on Cabin 3 until Madd picks her up at 6am.

Dallas: *Of course. Send her over. I'll keep an eye on her.*

Thanks, Ma.

Dallas: *Gunner. Don't do anything stupid.*

I turned off the phone as—

"Gunner?"

I turned to see a naked goddess leaning against the doorframe. Although she wasn't smiling.

Nerves swirled, my brain spun trying to decide what to do. What to say.

To stay, or not to stay.

"Is everything okay?" The look in her eyes told me she knew. She knew exactly what was happening. I watched her cross the room, in a kind of slow motion like I was wanting to soak up the last few seconds between us.

My pulse raced, an inner turmoil shaking me to my very core.

She stopped in front of me. I looked away in fear that I'd crumble.

In a tone as cold as ice, she said—

"You found him, didn't you? Gunner. Look at me. *Look* at me."

I forced myself to look her in her eyes. I owed her that much.

"Gunner..." Tears filled her eyes.

My heart shattered right there on the hardwood floor.

"Please. *Please* don't go. Don't do this. Call the cops. Let them handle..."

I had to get out of there. One second more and I'd cave. I took a step back.

"Pack your bag, Lexi."

"No. Gunner, *no,* please—"

"Pack your bag," I snapped and turned away. "I'll meet you outside in two minutes."

I forced one foot in front of the other until I made it out the front door. The night was icy cold against my sizzling skin. I took a deep breath, my lungs constricting along with my heart.

It has to be this way, I kept repeating in my head.

It has to be this way.

I would *not* take her down with me.

She didn't deserve that.

And I sure as hell didn't deserve her.

I'd just started the ATV when the front door flung open, popping on its hinges. With a bag over her shoulder, Lexi stomped down the stairs. She wasn't crying or pleading, she was pissed off.

She slid into the passenger seat and I hit the gas to ensure there was no room for conversation. To ensure I wouldn't break down and get back into bed with her.

That I was strong enough to let her go.

I rolled to a stop in front of the main house.

A moment slid by.

"This is really happening?"

I couldn't look at her.

"Gunner, I'm never going to see you again, am I?"

I clenched my jaw, willing my swirling stomach to ease with my heartbeat.

Another minute passed with her gaze cutting into the side of my face.

"Dallas is inside waiting for you. Go."

She jerked herself out of the ATV, taking my only moments of peace with her. Taking the light with her. The hope. The happiness. Taking *me* with her. I'd never fought an internal battle like that. Not even on the battlefield.

I pressed the gas.

"Gunner, no! Please!"

My hands gripped the steering wheel. Her pleas faded behind me but not until after I heard...

"I love you."

20

GUNNER

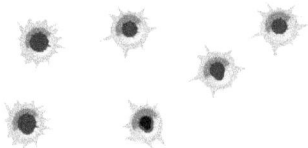

The fluorescent light flickered above us, spotlighting the black and white printout of the cabin's quadrants where we suspected the Knight Fox to be. The shooting range was dark, quiet, cold. Wolf, Ax and I hovered over the map, while Gage paced back and forth behind us like a tiger in a cage. An undercurrent of energy vibrated between us, that amped up adrenaline that builds before going into a war zone.

"Wolf, you take point here." I marked an X at the tip of a bluff. "You see anyone, or any movement at all, let us know."

He nodded.

I ran the tip of my pen along the map. "We'll park here, head out on foot, then split up here, at the dip of the valley. Then, Ax, you'll take the east side of the cabin, Gage, west, and I'll come up from the south."

"What's to say the area isn't rigged?"

I shook my head. "It's hunting season. No way Fox could get away with that."

"He could have cameras up."

"He could. Or, maybe he doesn't." It was something I'd

already considered. Bottom line, I'd decided it was a risk I was willing to take.

Thunder rumbled in the distance, rattling the steel door beside us. We turned, Ax's hand sliding to his gun, assessed, then refocused on the map.

"I've been to that cabin before," Wolf said. "It's been abandoned for decades. Old hunter's cabin. The roof is barely holding up. If I recall, it's got one room, two boarded windows, two doors. One in the front, one on the side. No electricity, running water, nothing."

"And it's only a few miles from where Fox killed Bear."

"Where's Cabin 3?" Ax asked me.

I kept my gaze on the map. "At the main house. With Dallas."

"And you're sending her to—"

"Yes. Madd will be here at oh six hundred to take her to Colorado and take over her case."

A moment ticked by. "That's a good decision, brother." Nothing got past Ax, ever.

"Alright guys," I cleared my throat. "To reiterate, this is strictly surveillance right now. We need to know exactly who and what we're up against. The Knight Fox took out dad, Feen, and he has Celeste, so he obviously knows what he's doing. We'll survey the area, then regroup in an hour at the rendezvous point here." I pointed to the valley where a few caves would provide shelter. "Then, we'll make a plan based on the surveillance and breech the cabin just before sun up. Got it?"

Nods around the room.

"Alright, suit up."

The familiar sound of metal against metal clinked through the air as we pulled on our vests, strapped on guns, ammo, knives, comms, night vision goggles. The motions sending a tingle in my balls I hadn't felt in years. Not since leaving the military.

I felt alive. Like I was doing something with my life. Like I had a purpose.

This was finally going to end.

"What about Jagg and Dallas? Did you tell them?" Gage strapped on a cross bow. Not sure what he planned to do with that, but whatever.

"No. Just us." I turned to Wolf. "To be clear, you're only part of the surveillance. After we regroup, I want you to head back to the main house. Make sure Dallas and Lexi are safe and stay that way."

Wolf shook his head. "No way man. Where you guys go, I go." He looked at each of us. "You guys are like brothers to me. Jesus, we fought next to each other in battle. Watched our brothers die. Fuck you, Gunner, I'm in."

I slowly stepped forward, leveling Wolf. My brothers shifted behind me.

"Hear me, Wolf. This is our cross to bear, it's *my* cross to bear. My dad, my brother, my sister. Mine. Mine to avenge. Mine to end. You will go back before we breech. Got it?"

The room fell silent, with only the pitter patter of the rain against the windows.

Finally, Wolf nodded and took a step back.

I turned to my brothers.

Ax handed me the bag.

I nodded and unwrapped the red velvet sheath and gripped the handle of the 1836 Colt Paterson Revolver that Phoenix had purchased years earlier. It was his most prized firearm.

It would be the gun I would use to kill the Knight Fox.

I slid the pistol into my holster, that cool, calmness flowing over me as it did moments before going into battle.

"Saddle up, guys."

We filed out, each taking off on our respective ATVs. The rain had become a steady deluge, making the moonless night as black as ink. Perfect for a midnight op.

I forced myself to push Lexi away, to quit wondering what she was doing, that she was okay. To forget the guilt I felt for letting her down.

Just another drop in the bucket, I told myself.

Except this one, I fucking loved.

God*damn* the irony of it all.

I kept my head on a swivel as I drove through the thick underbrush, knowing each tree like the back of my hand.

This was my land.

Gage and Ax were already at the valley when I pulled up.

"Where's Wolf?"

"Headed up to the cliff on the four wheeler. The sound of the engine won't carry through this rain."

I nodded.

For a second, we stared at each other, the meaning of the moment weighing down the air around us. Gage pulled a flask from his vest, unscrewed the top and held it up.

The initials D.E.S. reflected in the dim ATV headlights.

Duke Edward Steele.

"For Dad," he tipped it back, then handed it to Ax.

"For Feen." Ax took a swig, handed it to me.

"For revenge." I said, and took mine. "Gage, east; Ax, west; me, south. One hour, meet back here. See you on the other side, brothers."

With that, we split off on foot, stalking through the night as we had done so many times before. I pulled down my night vision and broke out in a jog. I wanted to be the first one there, to assess the danger before my brothers were close. Because if I knew anything about the Knight Fox, it was that he was prepared. Skilled.

Heartless.

With that thought, I pushed into a sprint, running through the woods like a deer, my heart beating like a war drum.

Yes, something was going to happen tonight.

Something was going to end.

21

LEXI

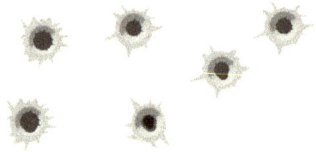

I wiped the rain from my face. I couldn't see a *thing* in front of me. The low growl of the ATV I'd swiped from Gunner's garage vibrated under my soaked legs. I tried to look past the pool of yellow light from the headlights, but there was nothing but blackness around me.

I was lost. Officially don't-know-up-from-down *lost*. Lost somewhere deep in the mountains.

When Gunner had left me standing at his front door, my heart had shattered. Watching the man I love going on a kamikaze mission was unbearable. I couldn't let it happen. So, I'd bypassed the house, dipped into the garage, stolen an ATV and took off toward the cabins. That's when I saw taillights in the distance. I followed them without hesitation, my desire to save Gunner overcoming all rational thought. I'd followed the ATV for at least twenty minutes, until I'd lost it somewhere past the dip of a mountain.

Yeah, I was *lost*.

I looked around the dense woods that surrounded me, miles and miles of mountains, miles of darkness. I couldn't even remember the direction I'd come from.

Nerves knotted my stomach as I looked over my shoulder for the hundredth time.

A shiver caught me. I was soaking wet with no dry clothes, no shelter. If the temperature continued to drop, I'd very likely suffer hypothermia.

I needed to move.

So I pressed on, maneuvering through the rocky terrain until I came to a deep valley that I hadn't seen before. After another glance around, I decided to head south, hoping to meet up with the dirt road that skirted around the Steele property.

At least thirty more minutes passed as I drove deeper and deeper into the woods, each minute getting colder, more anxious, more desperate to find either Gunner, or a way out of that endless darkness. Just then, the trees opened up to a small clearing with a dilapidated cabin in the middle.

Not a light on, no car, no road, not a soul around. Dead leaves scattered the front porch, rotted boards blocked the windows, a bare oak tree stretched like witches' fingers over the roof. Creepy, no doubt about that. But if I knew Gunner—and if he made it out of his mission alive—he'd come looking for me. He'd search every mountain until he found me, knowing I'd seek shelter somewhere. That cabin would be my refuge until Gunner found me, or until daybreak.

With that thought, I turned off the ATV and crossed the clearing.

∼

Gunner

. . .

I stopped cold at the sound of a four wheeler in the near distance. Wolf was on the cliff, my brothers on foot. Who the hell was on an ATV? Then, the engine went silent. I picked up my pace until I came to the edge of the woods beside the cabin. Movement to the north told me that I wasn't the only one surveying the abandoned building.

I clicked on the comm on my shoulder.

"Gage, Ax, Wolf, verify that you are not on the north side of the cabin."

"Affirmative."

"Affirmative."

"Dude, how the fuck did you get there so fast?" That one from Gage.

I clicked off, narrowed my eyes and watched the dark silhouette slink from tree to tree. After a moment, the figure darted across the clearing to the cabin.

My stomach fell to my feet. I knew that body, I knew those curves, I knew that long, brown hair.

Lexi.

I grabbed my comm.

"Wolf, need you to contact Dallas and make sure Lexi is there with her."

Crackle, crackle. "Will do, boss."

"Right *now*, Wolf."

A second ticked by, my attention laser focused on the cagey silhouette pressed up against the cabin.

"She's not answering."

"Try the main line."

A minute that felt like an hour stretched by.

Finally, "She's not there."

"What do you mean she's not there? I just talked to her."

"Well, I just talked to Opal..."

"Yeah?"

"She said Dallas hasn't been home all evening."

22

LEXI

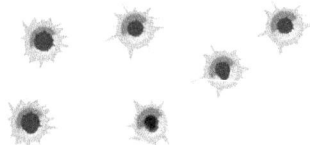

My heart hammered as I slammed my body up against the side of the cabin. I felt raw, exposed. Helpless.

But I was out of options.

After taking a few deep breaths, I crept around the corner, keeping my eyes and ears peeled.

I crouched under the boarded window, the drum of rain around me drowning out any potential noises inside.

With my fingertips on the cracked windowsill, I peeked through the wooden slats. A dim, bluish glow flickered from deep inside.

Someone was in there. I ducked down and crab walked to the front door.

Knock or run?

Knock or run?

My knees wobbled as I pushed to a stance. I reached for the knob, but the door opened.

. . .

And before I could scream, a hand wrapped around my nose and mouth and dragged me inside.

23

GUNNER

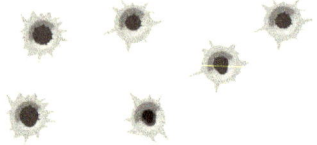

My heart slammed against my ribcage as I watched Lexi get pulled into the cabin.

I grabbed my comm. "ETA?"

"'Bout a half a klik."

"Same."

"Just set up on the cliff."

"Get your asses here now. I'm going in and I'm gonna need backup."

"What?"

"Can you repeat—"

"What the f—"

Their words faded as I ripped the night vision goggles off my head and pulled my gun. There was no waiting, no thinking, no planning as I took off through the clearing, the rain pounding my face.

I pressed my back against the cold, log wall, steadied my breathing and listened. Shuffles, whimpers, a few bangs sounded from inside. My pulse roared in my ears, my mind spinning to devise a plan I hadn't anticipated.

It would be at least a few minutes until Gage and Ax got there. Lexi didn't have a few minutes. Hell, if I knew anything about the Knight Fox, Lexi didn't have a few seconds.

I slid my hand over the trigger, edged around the building and paused at the front door. Double-fisting my gun, I took a quick inhale, then kicked through the door.

My eyes darted around the horror show in front of me. The scene was nothing like I'd ever seen before, not even in the darkest shadows of Afghanistan. In the corner of the barely lit room was Celeste, passed out cold on a cot with an IV drip in one arm. Her skin was grey, waxy. Her lips blue. The smell was reminiscent of every hostage raid I'd led.

I swung my gun around and my blood ran cold.

There are few times in your life that something will happen to you that is so out of left field, that is so unexpected, it changes the very course of your life. Changes? Hell, obliterates everything you thought you knew.

That was my time.

The gleam in Dallas's eyes matched the spark of the blade she held to Lexi's throat.

"Took you long enough," my stepmother said. The woman who'd raised me since I was a toddler.

My aim wavered as my brain struggled to catch up.

Dallas was the Knight Fox.

Our own stepmother was the Knight Fox.

The shock of it was second only to the rage that spurted through my body like a hot, burning acid.

"You killed my father."

Dallas's bloodshot eyes narrowed to slits against her flushed face. Her usually perfect hair was a tangled mess. She wore a black long-sleeved shirt, army fatigues, and combat boots. Around her waist, a belt of guns and ammo. She looked nothing like the domestic goddess I knew. Dallas looked like a special ops solider if I'd ever seen one.

"Killing your father was the cost of war, Gunner. You understand that."

"You're a Russian spy, aren't you. You're the Knight Fox."

Lexi closed her eyes, tears streaming down her cheeks.

"Surprised it took you so long to figure out, to be honest." Dallas said with a hint of a smirk. "When I'd married your father, I hadn't expected each of his sons to grow up to be special operators. Each of you overlooked it, except Phoenix, of course."

"And you tried to kill him when he figured it out." My finger tightened around the trigger. "Made it look like a suicide."

A hint of sadness crossed Dallas's face. "It hurt me to do that, Gunner. If you believe it or not, it hurt me."

"Did it hurt you when you killed Dad?" My voice vibrated.

"No." Her tone was ice cold. "I'd been groomed to be your father's wife since I was an orphaned pre-teen selling my soul in the slums of Moscow. I was picked to wed the director of the United States NSA when I became of age, no matter who that was." She shook her head. "That man was too smart for his own good. Duke figured out I was the one who assassinated Andrei Sokolov, the head of the SVR, a man whose radical ideas threatened everything Russia stood for. I had to take care of it. Of him. Of your dad. Incredible what you can do with altering heart medicine dosage."

"What does Celeste have to do with this?"

"That little walking file cabinet put together the fact that

I had traveled to Russia the week before Sokolov was killed. So, I had to deal with her." She laughed. "I took Wolf's new Harley to her house hoping to set him up for the fall."

"Why didn't you just kill her like you did everyone else?"

"Leverage. Once you all started figuring things out, I knew I needed something in case you came after me." She nodded to Lexi. "Now I have two things."

The knife in her hand shifted, followed by a thin trickle of blood down Lexi's neck. Everything faded at that point, Dallas, the revelations, everything funneled into one goal.

"Let Lexi go. She's not part of this, Dallas. Let her go."

"She became part of it when she began surveilling my partner."

"Bear."

"What a waste he was. Messy. Couldn't even handle taking out Lexi. I've had my eye on Lexi since she began her assignment. You see, we're everywhere, Gunner. Trust me, *everywhere.*"

I took a step forward. "Let her go."

"Lower your gun, Gunner, or I'll send this knife through her jugular and you'll watch her bleed to death on the floor."

"Wrong." I shook my head. "I'll be too busy gutting you."

"Drop the gun and kick it to me."

Lexi whimpered as Dallas pressed the knife harder against her throat.

With my gaze on Lexi, I lowered the gun and kicked it to Dallas's feet.

"Good boy. You were my tough kid, no doubt about that, but you always were my favorite. Had a grit that most others don't."

"You're a lying sack of shit, Dallas, and I'm going to drink every night to the fact that you're rotting away in prison somewhere."

A rush of cold air at my back told me Gage and Ax had breached.

"Guns down, boys, kick them over here."

A second passed.

"Weapons down, now!" Dallas screamed, her cool, calm demeanor shifting.

"Put 'em down, guys." I said. "Now."

Seconds later, a bevy of guns slid across the floor next to me, stopping at Dallas's feet.

She kicked them out of reach and started backing up, dragging Lexi with her. "You see, Gunner, I won't spend the rest of my life in jail. It's gone too far. My mission had ended with one final order. To end my life." Her hand began to tremble. "But not before I—

I lunged forward, ripping Lexi from her arms.

"Stop!" Dallas shrieked. She raised her other hand, each of us zeroing in on the grenade between her fingers.

I shoved Lexi behind me.

"This entire cabin is rigged to blow," Dallas's voice shook, her face contorted with rage. "Once I pull the pin, we're gone. All of us. Blown to pieces. Together."

They say that before you die, your life flashes before your eyes. Mine didn't. All I could see were my brothers, the love of my life, and my sister, Celeste. Five lives about to be cut short, one life who should have ended this a long time ago.

Dallas gripped the pin. "See you in hell, boys."

And that's when everything went into slow motion. The back door swinging open, the rain and dead leaves swirling inside. A flash of lightning illuminating a large, hooded silhouette stepping into the doorway.

. . .

And my brother, my hero, Phoenix, sending a bullet into the back of Dallas's head.

24

LEXI

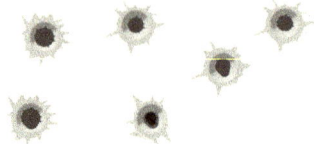

Six days later...

𝒩erves rippled through me as I glanced at the clock. Five minutes. I squatted down and checked the casserole bubbling away in the oven.

I hoped it was good.

Hell, I just hoped it was decent.

The hum of a motorcycle sent my nerves exploding. I looked at the clock again—four minutes early—and shook my head. Of course he was early. Gunner Steele was never late.

I spun around and checked my reflection in the microwave door. Instead of smoothing my hair or checking my teeth, I took three deep breaths.

I can do this, I kept telling myself.

Don't look down, I can do this.

A maniacal giggle burst out of me. I could *not* believe what I was doing.

After five days of laying low in Cabin 3 "until the smoke cleared" as Gunner had demanded, I was more than ready to do something outrageous, crazy, totally out of character.

Although I told myself I wasn't going to, I looked down at my freshly washed and shaven, stark-raving naked body wobbling on six-inch, platinum red heels.

Oh my *God*.

Boots up the porch steps outside…

I grabbed my wine and chugged the rest of the glass.

Liquid courage, liquid courage, liquid courage…

A brief knock before the knob turned. Of course he didn't wait, that jerk. He did own Cabin 3, after all.

I grabbed the short glass of whiskey I'd poured for him, dropped in one of those fancy square ice cubes, said a Hail Mary, and stepped out of the kitchen—ass naked, red heels, holding nothing but two fingers of Johnnie Walker Blue.

And I wished I could have gotten a picture of the look on his face.

Dressed in jeans, a white T-shirt under a black leather jacket and cowboy boots, Gunner stopped on a dime, his mouth gaping open with an almost child-like awe as he skimmed me from head to toe.

Butterflies tickled my stomach.

"Good evening," I said, in my most sultry voice. And yes, I'd practiced it in the bathroom mirror earlier that day. "Your four course meal awaits, my darling."

His eyes widened followed by a lopsided grin. "Four courses?" His focus zeroed between my legs. "I only need one, sweetheart."

"Oh, no, no, no, dear." Feeling a renewed confidence now, I sauntered over, took the phone and keys from his hand and set them on the side table. "Real food before dessert."

He pulled me into his arms. "Dessert now."

"No." I shoved away from his chest, my boobs jiggling just enough to make me blush. "Follow me, my dear."

I turned, revealing my backside to him. With bubbles of excitement in my stomach and a grin across my face the size of Texas, I led him into the kitchen, my hips giving a little extra sway.

No, I could not believe what I was doing. It felt exciting, *exhilarating*.

"Sit," I demanded with a wink.

"Lexi York, I'd jump off a building right now if you asked me to." He sat at the table where I'd arranged a placemat with gold-plated china that I'd borrowed from the main house, all the correct silverware, and a pair of glowing candles that matched the red of my heels.

I kneeled down in front of him and removed each boot, having to swat his hands away from my breasts four separate times.

After setting the boots aside, I retreated to the counter and began plating the dinner I'd practiced three times. Literally, *three* times.

"First course, bacon and leek soup."

Those indigo irises sparkled. *"Bacon?"*

"Yes, sir."

He held up his hands as if to surrender. "You naked, bacon in a bowl, and you just called me sir. I'm going to need you to bend over right now." He stood and started to undo his belt.

"No. *Sir*. Dinner first." I winked.

"Alright, alright, alright." He sank back down. "Good God, woman. You must be trying to kill me."

I served him soup, taking care to dip my nipples onto his cheek as I set the bowl on the table.

He nipped. It hurt—and kinda turned me on.

Then, I served myself and sat across from him in a wooden chair that felt like a block of ice underneath my ass.

He eyed me, the heat palpable.

"No," I repeated. "Food first, dear."

After a shake of his head, he dug in.

I waited on pins and needles...

"Holy *shit,* this is delicious."

... and felt like I'd won the lottery.

"You made this?"

"Well thanks for that slap in the face."

"I'd rather slap that ass. Seriously, you made it?"

"Yes." After three batches went down the garbage disposal but I didn't tell him that.

"I thought you said you couldn't cook."

"Well, turns out, it's really just following a recipe." I watched him devour the soup, a bit of color beginning to revive his sallow, stressed face. I realized then that I liked taking care of him. There was a pride, a happiness, that filled me. It filled my heart to be the one to revive him back to life. Help him relax, help him escape, help him be happy.

I rose from the table, walking on air. "Next course..." I picked up the plates from the counter. "BLTs."

"I'm going to marry you."

I grinned, set the plate in front of him. "Well, be forewarned that I'm not eating bacon for every meal for the rest of my life."

He bit into the sandwich—the Steele brothers' favorite dish—groaned and closed his eyes.

I nibbled mine until he was done.

"Third course," I pulled the dish from the oven. "Bacon hash brown casserole."

"No." He pushed away from the table. "We *are* getting

married, we *are* having bacon every day, but not until I fuck you until you can't remember your own name."

"Well that's romantic and all, but I want you to eat. You need to eat. Also, I want to hear about your day." I cleared my throat. "About Phoenix."

Well if there was anything to crush a raging boner, that was it.

He looked down, nodded, then slid back into his seat and took a hefty sip of whiskey.

We both took a bite of casserole—it was damn good—and after another sexual innuendo that I was pretty sure was illegal in several countries, we addressed the elephant in the room.

"Tell me. How is he?"

Gunner swallowed, wiped his mouth with his napkin. "Fighting with the entire medical staff."

I blew out a breath. What I had seen of Phoenix in the last few days was a stubborn raging bull whose emotions were a swinging pendulum between rage and confusion.

It had been hell on the family.

"How long are they going to keep him at the hospital?"

"Doc said he'll be released soon. Said it was nothing short of a miracle that he made it to the cabin and did what he did—that he even had the mental clarity, control, aim, strength to do it."

"I still can't believe that guy ripped out his IVs and busted out the window of his room."

"I can." Gunner took another sip. "Feen had heard everything, including Dallas's admission of everything right before heading to the cabin to kill herself, and us. Doc said he'd been awake the last few days and had been able to hear. Between you and me, me and my brothers wonder if he was playing deaf and dumb until he figured out a plan to get out."

"Why didn't Dallas kill him in the hospital?"

"Either she thought he wasn't going to survive, or, if he did, she probably thought he'd be incapacitated for the rest of his life—like everyone else did. Or it was just too risky. I assume the latter."

I sighed, shook my head.

Gunner stared at his food a moment, before diving back in.

I sipped my drink and let him eat, let him escape.

The story had hit national news, catapulting the Steele family into a world-wide spotlight. Dallas—real name Ana Lebedev—had been part of a massive foreign espionage ring that would undoubtedly take years to unravel. Not that the brothers cared much about that, all they cared about was that the woman was gone and their father's death had been avenged.

Gunner, along with his brothers hadn't left Phoenix's side since they'd forced him back into the hospital. Although I guessed it had more to do with making him stay, rather than their concern for his overall well-being.

The week had taken its toll, and I wanted to do everything I could to take an ounce of weight off Gunner's shoulders.

I also had news.

"I spoke with Astor today."

His gaze lifted from the fork-full he was about to shovel in his mouth.

"He offered me my job back, along with a promotion."

Gunner set down his fork, picked up his drink and drained the rest. I wasn't sure if that was a good thing or a bad thing.

"You're going to become an agent?" His face was blank, controlled.

I shifted in my seat. "Would you care?"

He stared at me for a full minute. "Yes."

"Why?"

"Because I don't want you to be in a job that could hurt you again. Because I love you, Lexi." He said it so black-and-white, with such strong conviction, such confidence, that I was speechless.

He stood, kicked the chair aside and kneeled at my feet.

He took my hands.

"I love you, Lexi. I've loved you from the moment I saw you. You're mine. I feel it in my gut. I'm not good at this whole relationship thing, but I will be. For you. I'll do whatever it takes. If you'll let me." He kissed my hand, like a knight to his princess, then looked up at me with that childlike excitement. "I want you to work for us, for Steele Shadows, here. Not just because I love you, but because you're smart, and you have the skill set we'd hire regardless that I love you. And you're one hell of a shot, which, apparently is necessary to work for us. Celeste wants to become a bodyguard full time. Says she wants to use her near-death experience to help others. She can, and she will. So we need an office manager to fill her space. I've already spoken with the boys. We'll pay triple anything Astor could offer. It's yours if you want it." His grip tightened on my hands. "I'm yours if you want me. Please let me. Give me a chance to be the man I know I can be. Give me the chance to be a good man."

I gripped his head in my hands. "You already are. I love you, Gunner Steele, just as you are, I love you. I'm yours. I'm *so* yours." Tears filled my eyes. "I'm in this for the long haul, by your side, through thick and thin."

"Perseverance."

"You haven't seen anything yet." I sniffed, kissed his head. "And by the way, I was going to say no to Astor, anyway."

"Really?"

"Yeah." I glanced down at my mom, Lola, tattooed on my arm. "I couldn't part with my tat."

His eyes glistened as he wrapped me into his arms and lifted me from the chair, cradling me like a baby.

"It's time for dessert, Lexi York."

"Wait." I stretched behind him and grabbed the cool whip from the counter.

"*Now* it's time for dessert."

And with one red heel dangling from my freshly painted toenail, he carried me into the bedroom and made me forget my own name.

25

GUNNER

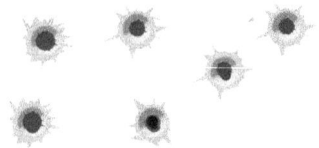

Three hours later...

I rounded the corner, barreling into Gage, who was babbling like an idiot on his damn cell phone.

A nurse giggled as she walked by.

"Jesus man, heads up."

"Yo, gotta call you back." Gage said into the phone before clicking off. "That was Jagg. He's swinging by."

"Good, maybe he can help knock some sense into Feen. How is he?"

"Clawing at the walls, dude."

"Did the doctor come by?"

Gage nodded to the window. We stepped into the shadowed corner of the lobby.

"Yeah, he came by. Says Feen's anger, confusion and disorientation is normal, and should subside as weeks go on."

"Weeks?"

"Yeah. He said to expect inconsistent behavior, mood swings, irritability—"

"So, nothing new."

Gage snorted. "Try amped up a few thousand notches. Said recovery for any kind of traumatic brain injury is usually around six months. Joked that we should put him in a padded room till then. Although I don't think he was really joking."

Neither of us laughed.

"What about the memory loss?"

"He shows significant signs of it. Doc says it may or may not come back with time. But…"

Gage's tone had my spine straightening.

"His fine motor skills are damaged. Bad." He shook his head. "Little things like zipping a zipper, brushing his teeth, even holding a drink for a long period of time, things like that, are going to be difficult for him. Obviously anything with a weapon is out of the question."

"For how long?"

Gage shrugged. "He'll need to be in physical therapy for months, at the very least."

"No way."

"Yeah."

I scrubbed my hands over my face. Phoenix agreeing to PT was like a fish agreeing to live in the desert. Even if we dragged him there, his participation would be nil. *Especially* with the amped up "inconsistent behavior, mood swings, and irritability."

It was the miracle of all miracles that our brother was in the condition he was after a bullet had lodged into his brain. But somehow, I didn't think *he* was going to look at it like that.

Gage continued. "I've got a list of drugs they want to put him on. Anti-depressants, anti-anxiety, sleep pills, the works."

"Shit."

"I know. Pretty sure the nurse snuck a valium in with his vitamins at lunch."

"Classy."

"Necessary."

We both stared down the long, white hallway that led to our brother's room. A minute stretched out between us as we tried to absorb what our new normal was going to be.

A pair of cops strode by.

"Nothing's changed, right?"

Gage shook his head. "Nope. It was self-defense. No charges will be filed against Feen. Doc did say though that they'll pull his licenses—his driving and concealed carry—until he completes a full mental evaluation. I think there's going to be a lot of couch time with a psychologist."

I shook my head. The hits kept coming. Feen was going to be thrown into physical and mental therapy—which would only be as helpful as his willing participation—and stripped of his independence. None of this was going to be a good thing, *for anyone.*

Gage's phone rang.

"Gotta take this. You alright?"

"Yeah."

He wiggled his eyebrows. "Yeah?"

"Yeah."

Gage winked. "I like her. Don't screw it up."

"I won't," I said, and realized I meant it.

After Gage disappeared outside, I made my way to Feen's room. I opened the door to a nurse muttering *"asshole,"* before barreling into my chest. She backed up, froze, her eyes rounding like golf balls.

"I'm so *sorry,* I—"

"You should see him without any meds."

She smiled, looked down, then skirted past me with reddening cheeks.

I closed the door behind me, my eyes locked on the dark silhouette standing in front of the window. Phoenix stood motionless, staring into the moonless night. His fists were clenched at his sides, his shoulders tense, every muscle in his body wound like a rubber band.

I knew he heard me. He didn't move.

My gut clenched watching him.

I had my brother back. For that, I was forever grateful, and forever indebted to the powers that be. But somehow, I knew he wasn't going to be the same guy I once knew.

I won't say I wasn't worried about the path that laid before Phoenix, but one thing I did know was that no one was tougher, no one was more determined, *no one* had a better chance of picking up the broken pieces than my brother, Phoenix Steele.

Even if we had to do it for him.

DON'T MISS THIS EXCITING NEWS

Dear Reader,

First and foremost, thank you for reading Steele Shadows Security! These three books are, by far, my favorites of all that I've written... and because of that, I've decided that I

can't let it go. You see, in the first draft of Cabin 1, Feen died. Yep, I killed him off. But that decision kept me up at night, along with the uproar from my Beta readers. So I went back to the table, rewrote Cabin 1, and kept Phoenix alive... and I'm SO GLAD I did because the ****unbreakable, badass Steele brother is getting his own standalone book.****
!!!!!!!!!!!

Are you as excited as I am?! **Phoenix (Steele Shadows Rising)** is now available for pre-order!!

That's not all... I'm thinking Astor, Wolf, Celeste, Jagg... they all deserve their own books. Don't you think?! Write in and let me know! Happy Reading! CHEERS!

*<u>Please note:</u> Phoenix and all forthcoming Steele Shadows books will be standalone steamy romantic suspense stories—**no cliffhangers!***

Don't forget to sign up for my newsletter to stay up to date on all things Steele Shadows! To make it super easy, you can simply **text AMANDABOOKS to 66866** to get automatically signed up!

Phoenix (Steele Shadows Rising)

**A man who cheated death.
A woman hired to pick up the broken pieces.
And an obsession strong enough to kill for.**

They told him he'd been given a second chance at life. Told

him to count his lucky stars, to stop and smell the roses. Kind of hard to do when your body is bound by chains and cuffs. That's what it felt like, anyway, when Phoenix Steele woke up from his coma to a life full of restrictions. Once known around town as the fearless, indomitable heir to the Steele fortune, the former Marine was suddenly labeled unstable, short-tempered, and loose cannon. Unwilling to accept his issues, Phoenix instantly clashes with his assertive therapist—the town's most eligible bachelorette.

No one knew overcoming the odds like Dr. Rose Floris. Determined not to be a statistic, Rose lived her life under carefully constructed routines—until a gruesome murder and a series of mysterious events reveal she's become the center of a madman's obsession. Suddenly, Rose's world is turned upside down and she finds herself under the watchful eye of her new patient, a broken man she's been warned not to trust.

As the tables begin to turn on their client-patient relationship, Phoenix realizes he must battle his own demons before he can save anyone, including the woman who's become his own obsession...

An obsession he'd kill for.

Grab your copy today!

SNEAK PEEK

Phoenix (Steele Shadows Rising)
Chapter 1

Rose

Lightning lit the sky, a momentary reprieve from the darkness of the kitchen around me. I twisted my long, black hair between my fingers, my eyes widening with the flash of light. A fear of what might be illuminated sending a chill colder than the temperature up my spine. I can still remember that moment. I was wearing my favorite purple nightgown, a pair of holey pink socks. The kind with the little pom pom ball on the back. Purple, to match the gown that hadn't been washed in weeks, but I didn't care. It was mine, it fit, and made me feel like a princess. Night after night, I'd pretend it was a glamorous gown and that I was trapped in a castle by an evildoer. A *really* evil one, with slitted red eyes, squared chin, pointed nails, the works. I still can't watch Nightmare on Elm Street. Heck, that movie might as well be a biography at this point, because Lord knew, I'd seen hell up close in that house. Evil, as sure as my beating heart, in human form. But dream after dream, no white knight came to save me. No one saved me. The crazy thing is, despite that, I continued to dream. Between matted lashes, swollen eyes, and years that dragged on, I still dreamed. Why? It's that little light that children carry inside them. The light that for some ignites a happy, fruitful path, but for others, dims or fades all together when the pain of the world around them becomes too great. Although the latter was my path, I continued to dream. Incredible thing, the human mind is. The spirit to thrive. To survive. Looking back, that little light was what saved my life.

A loud *pop* of thunder sent my heart slamming against my ribcage. Windows rattled above me. I hugged my knees to my chest, pressing my back against the wall, the thin sheetrock like ice through my nightgown.

I knew how fragile sheet rock could be.

I knew from experience.

Then, the sleet started. First, a delicate pitter patter, quickly turning into a loud buzz against the roof. You've probably heard of thunder snow before. This was thunder sleet. To this day, I've never seen weather like it. Typical early spring in the south. That year, winter desperately clutched on with its icy grip. Unrelenting.

I closed my eyes imagining the ice falling from the sky, sparkles of silver against streaks of lightning, carrying on the wings of the wind. Free to fall where it wanted, free to fly away.

Free to melt away in a silent surrender.

I imagined myself as that ice, fading away. Away from the pain, the torment, the life I'd been thrown into, the series of circumstances that shaped the woman I would become.

For better or worse.

The definition of evolution is the gradual development of something, from a simple form to a complex form. There are three main types of evolution: convergent, parallel, and divergent.

Convergent evolution occurs when species of different ancestors begin to develop similar traits in response to their habitat. Think of birds, insects, bats. Each very different species, but each sharing the ability to fly. Parallel evolution happens when two independent species evolve separately, without sharing any of the same traits or adaptations.

Divergent is the most commonly addressed and debated form of evolution. This happens when two species share the same ancestor but each gradually becomes different over time. The first study of divergent evolution dates back to 1895 when a young explorer named Charles Darwin visited the Galapagos Islands where he studied finches, noting how their beaks were different according to their diet. Same ancestor, but different species over time.

I, Rose Floris, was a walking example of divergent evolution. Of environment and predation pressures, or, the effects of being preyed upon.

Natural selection.

The weak are destroyed.

Only the strongest survive.

Adapt, or die.

I understood this concept from a very young age.

Sure, to most, evolution meant advancement, growth, progress. But for me, it was something deeper, something darker. A necessary adaptation to the environment I'd been thrown into.

My definition of evolution? A will to survive, no matter

age, circumstance, environment. And that will, I've learned, is the strongest part of the human body.

You might have heard of children being compared to clay. They can be molded and shaped at a young age with the end goal of becoming a productive, functioning adult. I remember watching children at the playground with their parents while mine left me in the car to make a quick run down the back alley. The gleeful giggles, the joy in the smallest things. Their prideful smiles as their parents cheered them down the slide. Appreciation for life, for family, for things.

Happiness—an adaptation of their environment.

Not for me. For me, my adaptation was silence. Fading into my environment so that I was neither seen nor heard. Becoming as much of "nothing" as I possibly could. It was a type of survival, and one that, unfortunately, goes overlooked.

In school, I learned very quickly that the misfits were the only ones who were assumed to have a difficult upbringing. The more rebellious the kid is, the more defiant, the more obnoxious and crude, the ones who get into physical altercations—those were the kids that had it worst at home. Not true. There was an entirely different species of children who had it much worse than little Johnny with the bloody knuckles.

Those were the quiet kids.

The ones in the shadows, in the corner. The ones who never made eye contact.

The ones with bruises under their clothes.

That was me.

To be silent, to *not* fight was to survive. A complacent acceptance manifesting in silence, while unrelenting anxiety churning inside your stomach evolves you into something else.

Yeah, I knew evolution all too well.

And that night, I witnessed the effects of environmental impact on human life. Natural selection? I sure hoped so.

The house had been quiet for hours. Cheryl had given up on looking for me sometime around sunset, as she usually did. Funnily enough, they never looked under the kitchen table, which had become my nightly refuge until they'd go to bed.

Rain began to mix with the sleet, a steady deluge, a white noise buzzing around me blocking out everything else. It was those moments that I took my chances. Few and far between, but I took them when I could. My gaze fixed on the refrigerator only a few feet away. Anxiety bubbled inside me, knowing that eating without approval would lead to another run in with the sheet rock. *Feed me more, then,* I'd think. Simple.

The rain picked up, pellets of ice sliding down the windows. My eyes darted from the doorway, back to the fridge, to the window, then back to the doorway.

Confident that the storm would block out any noise I'd make, I pushed away from the corner, maneuvering between the chairs under the dining table as I had done so many times. A snake, slithering through the darkness. More lightning, more thunder to drown out any mistake I might make.

A waft of cold air swept past me as I slinked out from under the table. I froze like a groundhog peeking up from the ground. Exposed, vulnerable.

But hungry.

I was *so hungry.*

It had been seventeen hours since I'd eaten—yes, I'd counted—a crust of a microwave pizza I'd been tossed. They liked to mess with me like that. A cliché power trip. I know that now.

My pulse hammered as I forced myself forward, shuffling on my knees along the cold, tiled floor. Stay low, stay small. Low so that they couldn't see you. Small, in case they did. The smaller the target, the harder to hit. Heck of a lesson for a child.

My hands trembled—I'm talking *earthquake* trembled—as I reached for the handle.

And that's when the front door flew open.

Lightning outlined his silhouette like the villain in every little girl's dream. Freddy, indeed. Rain swirled around his untied boots as he stumbled inside. I dropped to the floor, spun around and slammed my back against the cabinets, praying he didn't see me.

His scream was something out of a horror movie, echoing off the walls and lingering in the air as if to punctuate the shock.

I stilled, wondering what could entice that kind of reaction from a man who was the one who typically did the scaring.

Boots shuffled across the living room, a low, panicked repetitive muttering of something I couldn't make out. My thoughts spun, every instinct in my body telling me that something was wrong. Very, very wrong.

"Rose!" My name exploded from his lips. It wasn't the first time he'd screamed my name, but it was the first time it sounded like *that*.

"Rose!"

My heart kick started into panic mode, my gaze darting around the kitchen, stopping on the window above the sink. Could I make it? Could I escape?

"Rose!"

I surged to my feet, my nightgown catching and ripping on a nail sticking out from the cabinet.

My legs moved like rubber though the kitchen, a sick need to both see what was happening in the other room, and to prevent myself from another night in the emergency room after "falling down the stairs."

I stepped into the doorway of the living room.

A low, haunting melody accompanied the end of a movie streaming on the television. His back was to me, shuffling from side to side, frantic mumbles against the music.

And as my gaze shifted to the couch, my stomach plummeted.

That's when it happened.

That's when my life took a turn.

Natural selection. That was my personal theory, anyway. Because evil like that didn't have a place on earth. Evil like that faced its own demons.

And demons always win... unless you face them.

And I'd faced mine. That night, I'd faced mine.

I was eight years old.

Eight years old when I'd decided enough was enough.

PHOENIX (STEELE SHADOWS RISING)

**A man who cheated death.
A woman hired to pick up the broken pieces.
And an obsession strong enough to kill for.**

They told him he'd been given a second chance at life. Told him to count his lucky stars, to stop and smell the roses. Kind of hard to do when your body is bound by chains and cuffs. That's what it felt like, anyway, when Phoenix Steele woke up from his coma to a life full of restrictions. Once known around town as the fearless, indomitable heir to the Steele fortune, the former Marine was suddenly labeled unstable, short-tempered, and loose cannon. Unwilling to accept his issues, Phoenix instantly clashes with his assertive therapist—the town's most eligible bachelorette.

No one knew overcoming the odds like Dr. Rose Floris. Determined not to be a statistic, Rose lived her life under carefully constructed routines—until a gruesome murder and a series of mysterious events reveal she's become the center of a madman's obsession. Suddenly, Rose's world is turned upside down and she finds herself under the watchful eye of her new patient, a broken man she's been warned not to trust.

As the tables begin to turn on their client-patient relationship, Phoenix realizes he must battle his own demons before he can save anyone, including the woman who's become his own obsession...
An obsession he'd kill for.

Phoenix is a standalone romantic suspense (no cliff-hanger!)

★ BURIED DECEPTION ★

In the pulse-racing first installment of the On the Edge series, a criminal psychologist teams up with a former marine on a deadly wildland mission. Not even their hearts can stay out of harm's way.

PREORDER NOW

In the swamps of East Texas, alligators aren't the only danger lurking in the shadows.

After a young woman is brutally attacked on a popular hiking trail, the evidence points to the notorious Black Cat Stalker. The town of Skull Hollow enlists Dr. Mia Frost to provide a psychological profile and assist in the investigation.

When another person goes missing, Mia partners with Easton Crew, former marine and current CEO of a tactical tracking company. Both Mia and Easton are stubborn, strong-willed, and independent, but neither can deny the smoldering attraction between them.

As professional lines blur, Easton starts to question Mia's motives and worries she's getting too close to the investigation. The mystery begins to unravel, but so does Mia's mental health as the clues dredge up her own haunted past.

It soon becomes evident that things aren't as they seem … and people aren't always who they say they are.

Sign up for my newsletter to be the first to receive details on my next release...

ABOUT THE AUTHOR

Amanda McKinney is the bestselling and multi-award-winning author of more than twenty romantic suspense and mystery novels. Her book, Rattlesnake Road, was named one of *POPSUGAR's 12 Best Romance Books,* and was featured on the *Today Show.* The fifth book in her Steele Shadows series was recently nominated for the prestigious *Daphne du Maurier Award for Excellence in Mystery/Suspense.* Amanda's books have received over fifteen literary awards and nominations.

Text **AMANDABOOKS to 66866** to sign up for Amanda's Newsletter and get the latest on new releases, promos, and freebies!

www.amandamckinneyauthor.com

If you enjoyed CABIN 3, please write a review!

★ MORE BY AMANDA MCKINNEY ★

NARRATIVE OF A MAD WOMAN (THRILLER SERIES):
The Widow of Weeping Pines
The Raven's Wife
The Lie Between Her (Summer 2023)
The Keeper's Closet (Summer 2023)

ON THE EDGE SERIES:
Buried Deception
Trail of Deception (2023)

THE ROAD SERIES:
Rattlesnake Road
Redemption Road

#1 BESTSELLING STEELE SHADOWS:
Cabin 1 (Steele Shadows Security)
Cabin 2 (Steele Shadows Security)
Cabin 3 (Steele Shadows Security)
Phoenix (Steele Shadows Rising)
Jagger (Steele Shadows Investigations)
Ryder (Steele Shadows Investigations)
Her Mercenary (Steele Shadows Mercenaries)

THE AWARD-WINNING BERRY SPRINGS SERIES:
The Woods (A Berry Springs Novel)
The Lake (A Berry Springs Novel)
The Storm (A Berry Springs Novel)
The Fog (A Berry Springs Novel)

The Creek (A Berry Springs Novel)
The Shadow (A Berry Springs Novel)
The Cave (A Berry Springs Novel)

The Viper

Devil's Gold (A Black Rose Mystery, Book 1)
Hatchet Hollow (A Black Rose Mystery, Book 2)
Tomb's Tale (A Black Rose Mystery Book 3)
Evil Eye (A Black Rose Mystery Book 4)
Sinister Secrets (A Black Rose Mystery Book 5)

READING ORDER GUIDE

READING GUIDE

Dark Romance/Thriller

Romantic Suspense/Crime Thriller

↓ Romantic Suspense ↓

Romantic Suspense/Paranormal Novellas

   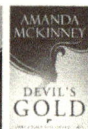 

READING GUIDE

↓ Psychological/Domestic Thriller ↓

The Widow of Weeping Pines: 12/02/22
The Raven's Wife: 1/20/23
The Lie Between Us: 6/30/23
The Keeper's Closet: 8/11/23

Thriller Standalone
Details coming soon!